Game On

—

Nancy Warren

D0053062

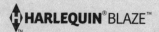
HARLEQUIN® BLAZE™

ISBN-13: 978-0-373-79789-9

GAME ON

Copyright © 2014 by Nancy Warren

Printed in U.S.A.

HARLEQUIN®
www.Harlequin.com

"I don't think this is going to be a strictly business relationship...."

Before Serena could respond, Adam closed the distance between them, pulled her to him and closed his mouth on hers. Hot, determined, possessive, his lips moved over hers. He gave her a moment to accept or reject his caress and she used that moment to angle her body closer, to open her lips in mute invitation.

He took her mouth then, licking into her, giving her a taste of his power and hunger. Which, naturally, incited her own power and hunger. And, oh, she was hungry. He reminded her of how long it had been since she'd lost herself in a man.

A tiny sound came out of her throat, half moan, half purr. He took that as encouragement and pulled her even closer, running his hands over her curves. She felt his arousal as he held her tight against his body, felt her own excitement building within her.

A car with all the windows open, music blasting, roared into the parking lot, and he quickly pulled away, shielding her with his body.

"Aha," he said.

She gazed up at him, stunned at the strength of her own response. "I don't date my clients," she reminded them both.

"I don't recall asking you for a date," he said, all sexy and pleased with himself.

"You're going to be trouble, aren't you?"

"Oh, I hope so...."

Blaze®

Dear Reader,

I have a friend, John, who is still best friends with two other guys he calls his "sandbox buddies" because they all met when they were kids. They lived in the same neighborhood, went to school together and are now grown men with families of their own. I find it amazing that these three are still close friends and are always there for each other. Of course, to a writer, anything interesting is likely to find its way into a book. In this case, three books.

My fictitious three heroes are all turning thirty-five. Gorgeous and successful, they still play games together. In this case, amateur hockey. They are also all still single, which becomes a bet to see who will remain so longest. Who will be the Last Bachelor Standing?

Adam Shawnigan is up first. He's a cop and also having a few performance issues on the ice. Adam's buddy Max sets him up—much against his will—with a performance coach to help him figure out why he chokes under pressure. Serena Long is in demand as a performance coach and professional speaker. She's really good at figuring out how and why people sabotage themselves. But in her real life, an anonymous "fan" is trying to sabotage her. How far will this cyber-stalker go? And can Adam stop him before it's too late?

I hope you enjoy *Game On* and watch for *Breakaway* and *Final Score* coming soon. Stop by to visit me on the web at www.nancywarren.net.

Happy reading!

Nancy Warren

ABOUT THE AUTHOR

USA TODAY bestselling author Nancy Warren lives in the Pacific Northwest, where her hobbies include skiing, hiking and snowshoeing. She's an author of more than thirty novels and novellas for Harlequin and has won numerous awards. Visit her website, at www.nancywarren.net.

Books by Nancy Warren

HARLEQUIN BLAZE

To get the inside scoop on Harlequin Blaze and its talented writers, be sure to check out blazeauthors.com.

Other titles by this author available in ebook format. Don't miss any of our special offers. Write to us at the following address for information on our newest releases.

Harlequin Reader Service
U.S.: 3010 Walden Ave., P.O. Box 1325, Buffalo, NY 14269
Canadian: P.O. Box 609, Fort Erie, Ont. L2A 5X3

Game On is dedicated to the three real-life sandbox buddies: John, Andrew and Bill.

You guys rock.

1

"HEY, DYLAN, GRAB the fire hose," Max Varo joked as the homemade chocolate cake laden with thirty-five burning candles made its way into the Shawnigan family rec room. The cake wobbled slightly in June Shawnigan's hands as she broke into a soprano rendition of "Happy Birthday to You." The fifty or so people singing along were assorted friends and family of Adam Shawnigan, June's baby, thirty-five today.

She suspected his surprise party hadn't been a surprise for more than a nanosecond—he was a detective, after all—but he was putting on a good face for the celebration.

It was a rugged, handsome face, too, if she did say so herself. She wasn't the only one who noticed. As she looked around, June could see the expressions on some of the younger women's faces. Adam was, as more than one young woman had informed her, a major hottie. So why was her thirty-five-year-old major-hottie son still single?

When he'd finished blowing out the candles, and she'd passed slices of cake and forks, she called for quiet and motioned to her husband, Dennis, to dim the lights and push Play.

"No. For the love of God, no," moaned Adam as the big-screen TV came to life. Oh, she'd surprised him now, she thought with satisfaction as the home movie she'd taken on her first camcorder thirty years ago filled the screen.

Three little boys sat at the picnic table in June's backyard, all chubby faces and mustard-stained mouths, chomping through hot dogs and potato chips. She must have guessed they'd stay still for at least another minute or two, so she'd grabbed her new camcorder, pushed Record. Of course, at five years old, the three were used to being followed around by eager parents with cameras and barely batted an eye.

She said, "Adam, how old are you today?"

"I'm five," he said, looking at the camera as though a not-very-bright woman were behind it.

"What do you want to be when you grow up?" she asked.

"I'm going to be a police officer," he said, dipping his hot dog into a pool of ketchup and stuffing it into his mouth. Even then he'd had big blue eyes that were so like his father's. Then, his mouth full, he mumbled, "Like my dad."

"Aw," said a chorus of voices in the living room.

"How about you, Dylan?" she asked the freckle-faced kid next to her son, as if his answer weren't perched on his head.

He put his hand on the red plastic firefighter's helmet he'd barely taken off in a year and said, "A fireman." Dylan was the tallest of the three boys and the most daring. It had come as no surprise to June when he'd been cited for bravery four years ago for rushing into a burning building as it collapsed to save a young woman's life.

"Amazing," a voice from the crowd piped up. "Who gets their career right at five?"

"What about you, Max?" she asked the smallest of the

three boys. Max Varo at five was very much like Max Varo at thirty-five. He had dark South American good looks and a neatly buttoned shirt that showed no signs of dropped food—unlike the shirts of the other two. He ate tidily and always remembered to say *please* and *thank you*. "I am going to be an astronaut."

"Or a billionaire," Dylan called out. There was general laughter in the crowded rec room but she couldn't help looking at Max now. He grinned at the crack, but June wondered how many people realized how bitterly he'd resented the childhood ear infection that had done enough damage to his hearing that becoming an astronaut—or even a commercial pilot—was never going to be possible.

But on-screen it was 1983 and everything was still possible. Because the boys were adorable—and she was of a matchmaking disposition—June then asked, "And who are you going to marry, Adam?"

Laughter and someone shouting, "Yeah, Adam, who are you going to marry?" almost drowned out the little boy's voice. On-screen he grinned at her and said, "Princess Diana."

"She's already married, stupid," Dylan informed him. Then, unasked, he said, "I'm going to marry Xena, warrior princess."

"How about you, Max?"

The serious little boy said, "I'm not getting married until I'm grown up."

She stopped the show there and as the party grew more raucous, she went over to her husband, who wrapped his arms around her. "A dead princess, a comic-book character and a boy who's waiting to grow up. No wonder they're all still single."

"Give them time, sweetie," Dennis said, kissing the top of her head.

"They're thirty-five—how much time do they need? I want to take movies of my grandchildren out on that picnic table before I'm too old and weak to hold a camera."

As though in answer, the three men, still best friends, all tough, loyal, gorgeous and as dear to her as though they were all her children, started one of their complicated bets, the rules of which were known only to themselves. But she wasn't so clueless she didn't see where this was going.

"Oh, no. Dennis, are they making a bet to see who can stay single the longest?"

Her heart began to sink as her husband solemnly nodded, and the three men clinked beer bottles. "To the last bachelor standing."

"I CAN'T DO IT," the man at the podium said into the microphone. As his admission of failure bounced through the air, he pushed the mic away with a grunt of frustration and stomped down two steps to throw himself into the seat beside Serena Long. Fortunately, she was the only person in the audience.

She'd decided to have her first session with Marcus Lemming in the auditorium of his gaming empire's brand-new headquarters here in Hunter, Washington.

"Okay," she said calmly. "You can't do it. You can't give a speech to your potential shareholders. What does that mean?"

Marcus wiped clammy sweat off his forehead with a trembling hand. Instead of answering her, the twenty-six-year-old CEO said, "I'm worth 100 million dollars. I'm a computer frickin' genius. And when I stand up there, I feel like I'll throw up."

"I know. That's why you hired me." She loved being a performance coach and she was damn good at it. "I want you to breathe into your fear."

He stared at her.

"Go on, breathe. Feel the energy, the raw power of that fear. Now, we're going to take that energy and turn it into positive excitement. You have a great site, a winning formula. No one can sell it like you can."

"Yeah. Online. I could write a killer email. Why can't the suits be happy with that?"

She laughed even though she suspected he was only half joking. Fear of public speaking was higher than fear of death on the stress scale to certain people. And she loved them for it. They were making her rich. "I guarantee that if you do the exercises and the work I assign you, in a month you will give that speech. I'm not saying you'll love every minute of it, but you'll speak in public and you will do fine."

"You guarantee it?"

"Yep."

"You're that good?"

She grinned at him. "Yep."

"I can't even give a speech to one person. How am I going to talk to hundreds, with a media feed broadcasting out to millions?"

"We start small. Okay. Maybe you're not ready for the mic and the auditorium yet. I'll get you some water. And then you'll sit here right beside me and read your speech."

"My speechwriter said it's lame to read a speech."

"Like I said, we start small."

By the time she left Marcus, he'd been able to read his speech to her without vomiting, crying or fainting. It was a start.

Serena was one of the best at what she did, coaching better performance out of employees, helping superstars fight their demons or overcome their handicaps, whether they struggled with public speaking, learning how to manage people or goal setting. She was part business tycoon, part psychologist and, as a client once suggested, part witch. She wasn't sure about the last part, but she did have instincts that surprised even her sometimes when she worked what appeared to be magic.

When Max Varo's name showed up on her call display as she was clicking open the door locks of her car, she answered her cell phone at once.

"Max," she said, letting the pleasure she felt out in her tone. "How are you?"

"Never better." He wasn't one to waste time, not his or hers, so he got right to the point. "I need a favor."

They'd met in Boston, when both took their MBAs, she with her human resources background, he with astrophysics and a few other degrees under his belt. She considered Max her first success in performance coaching. She hadn't even realized that was what she wanted to do until she helped him turn his life around and realized she could do the same thing for others.

They'd been friends ever since and he'd sent her some of her best clients. If he needed a favor, they both knew he was going to get it.

"What's up?"

"You know I play amateur hockey?"

"Sure."

"Well, our center forward is choking under pressure. He's a great player all year but when we get to the championships, he just freezes up."

"Performance anxiety," she diagnosed.

"I know. But we can't replace him. He's the best we've got, plus one of my closest friends. I need you to work with him, get him over this choking thing."

"I'm not a sports coach."

"Serena, you could get Bill Gates into the NBA if he wanted it."

"Okay. You have a point. But it's not really my field."

"Look at it this way. You won't get paid, so nobody's going to judge you."

She was as busy as she'd ever been, had recently turned down paying work in her chosen field, business, and now she was contemplating working pro bono for a sports guy? If it were anyone but Max...

"I don't know the first thing about hockey," she warned.

"You don't need to know about hockey. His problem isn't related to stick-handling skills. He's choking under pressure. Nobody helps a man struggling to find success like you."

"He'd better be super motivated."

"Adam Shawnigan is dying to work with you," he assured her. "I can't wait to tell him the good news after our game tonight."

ADAM LOVED HOCKEY. After a day of precinct coffee, discovering evidence he'd worked months to gather in a murder trial had been deemed inadmissible and getting yelled at by a woman who insisted her taxpayer dollars gave her the right to report her dog as a missing person, it felt good to step out onto the ice.

Out here the sound of a skate blade carving cold, clean tracks helped clear the crap out of his mind. With a stick in his hands and a puck to focus on, he had control over his destiny, even if only for a couple of hours.

Max and Dylan played alongside him, as they had since their parents had signed them up for hockey when they were in first grade. They'd all kept up the game and now played in the same emergency-services league. Most of the players were cops and firefighters, with a few ambulance guys thrown in. Max barely qualified since he was a reserve firefighter, but he paid for the uniforms, so the Hunter Hurricanes weren't inclined to complain.

Normally they practiced once a week at 5:00 or 5:30 a.m. and played a weekly game, but with play-offs looming, they'd upped their practice schedule and it showed. Well into the third period against the Bend Bandits, they were ahead 3–2. Adam was center forward. With Dylan and Max as wingmen, he felt they were a dream trio. They'd come close to bagging the Badges on Ice championship not once but twice. This time, he told himself. This year that cup was theirs. All he had to do was focus.

Max, the right wing, had the puck and stayed back while Adam and Dylan crossed paths and headed for the offensive zone in a classic forward crisscross they'd practiced hundreds of times. Max then shot a crisp pass to Dylan. They were gaining speed. Adam felt his adrenaline pump. Focus and timing were everything. Max maneuvered himself into the high slot. Dylan, under attack, passed to Adam, who flicked the puck to Max. But the goalie was right on him. Instead of taking the shot, Max tipped the puck to Dylan, who then sent the thing flying past the stumbling goalie and scored.

Magic. They were magic on ice. This year that championship was theirs, and nothing was getting in the way.

After the backslaps and congratulations, the shaking hands when the game was over, the teams headed for the change room. Max said, "Adam, hold up a second." Dylan hung back, too.

He listened in growing irritation as Max told him about the great "favor" he'd arranged.

"There is no damn way I am letting some bossy do-gooder inside my head," Adam snapped, sending puffs of white breath into the freezing air inside the rink.

"She's a performance coach. The woman's amazing."

"I don't need a performance coach. How many goals did I score this season?" He turned to glare at his two best friends.

"How about in play-offs last year?" Dylan asked.

The familiar churn began in his gut as it did whenever he thought about play-offs. "I had a stomach bug or something last year. That's why I was off my game."

"And the year before?"

His scowl deepened. "Maybe a case messed up my concentration. I forget."

"Dude, my grandma could have made the shot you missed last year. The net was open and you missed it! You choked," Dylan said. "It happens. But we want to win the championship this year. We all want it real bad."

"So do I!" What did they think? He was the team captain, center. Of course he wanted to win. All he needed to do was focus more. Somehow he'd lost his edge in the last two championship games. He wouldn't let it happen again.

"Then at least meet with Serena Long," Max said. "She's eager to work with you."

He scowled. Glared at both of them. "She'd better be hot."

2

SERENA SNUGGLED INTO her black wool jacket, wishing she'd thought to throw a parka into her car when she'd headed out into the early-morning darkness. Except that she didn't own a parka.

Or skis.

Or snowshoes.

Or a sled.

Or skates.

She didn't do winter if she could help it. And she certainly didn't get up at 4:45 in the morning in order to turn up at a freezing-cold rink by 5:30 a.m. to watch a bunch of grown men practice sliding around on the ice chasing a disk. And beating up on each other when they didn't get it.

The heels on her black boots clacked as she made her way to rink 6. Amazingly, all the rinks in the sportsplex seemed to be full. Sleepy parents with takeout coffees watched kids of all sizes slide around. It was amazing, an entire life that went on while she slept.

When she entered the practice rink Max had directed her to, there weren't any parents pressed up against the plexiglass looking sleep deprived. In fact, there were only

players on the ice and players on the bench. The small
seating area was empty.

She wasn't a hockey fan by any means, but she'd played
field hockey in school and figured the basic rules ought
to be similar. Max had told her he played right wing, and
yep, there he was, one of the smaller players on the ice.
The big guy in the middle would be Adam Shawnigan.

She watched him. They seemed to be working on some
kind of passing drill. She could feel the concentration of
the guys on the ice. With no crowd the sounds were mag-
nified—the scratch of skates, the smack of stick to puck,
the groaned obscenities when some guy missed the puck
completely.

WHEN THE TEAM came off the ice, she stayed where she
was, interested in studying the dynamics between the players. It was clear immediately that Adam was the leader.
Most everyone took the time to comment or joke as they
passed him. He had a good word, a laugh or a pat on the
back for all the guys. Max and he and a third man she assumed was Dylan, the left wing, remained standing after
the rest of the team had ambled away.

She rose and walked down the steps to join the group
of three, all of whom turned to watch her approach.

But she was aware of only one of them. The tallest one
in the middle.

Max had told her plenty about Adam Shawnigan. His
hockey record, his work experience—highlighting some
of the more dramatic cases he'd solved—even their childhood exploits.

What Max had neglected to tell her was that Adam
Shawnigan was like something out of mythology. Thor,
maybe, she thought, recalling the movie her nieces had
dragged her to. Gorgeous, tough, larger-than-life. Even

sweaty and unshaven, still breathing heavily from the last play, the man exuded sex appeal. When his eyes rested on her, she felt as though he could see all her secrets. It was both intriguing and a little uncomfortable. She preferred to keep her secrets until she felt like sharing them.

His eyes were an intense blue, not the twinkling happy kind but a hard blue that spoke of experiences and memories she was glad she didn't share. Even if she hadn't known he was a cop, she'd have guessed either law enforcement or military. Those eyes were watchful, checking her out while giving nothing away. His face was tough and rugged and needed a shave. He had a groove in his chin deep enough to rest a pencil in.

All of which made his mouth the most incredible surprise. Full lips that looked soft and sensitive. He held them in a rigid line, but it didn't help. Those lips were poutier than a supermodel's. And if she didn't stop staring at them, she was going to make a fool of herself.

She shifted her gaze to Max—sweet, comfortable Max—who immediately made introductions. "Adam Shawnigan, meet Serena Long. Serena's agreed to give you a few coaching sessions."

Adam opened his mouth, and she could see the words forming, something like *I don't need no stinkin' performance coach,* but then he glanced at Max and she could see they'd been down this road already. He paused, thumped one glove against the other and said, "Yeah. So I heard."

And this was the guy who was dying to work with her?

She glared at her old friend, got a slight shrug in return.

"When do you want to begin?" Max asked.

"Maybe in a couple of weeks," Adam said. "Closer—"

She interrupted immediately. He might be king of the rink, but he wasn't going to rule her. "I got up at 4:45 a.m. and drove all the way out here. I suggest we start now," she said. She was already giving up her time. She didn't intend to be dictated to by her charity case.

The charity case spluttered, "I've got work. I have to be in the office—"

"I'd really like thirty minutes of your time." She turned and began gathering her stuff.

Behind her she heard Max speak in a low voice, but not so low she couldn't hear—which, knowing Max, would be deliberate. "If you screw this up, we'll be changing the lines for the big game."

"Says who?"

"The whole team. We talked about it."

"Dylan?"

She imagined those big lips hanging open in shock.

Dylan said, "It's about the team. We all want to win this year. At least give her a try."

There was a pause so pregnant it must have contained triplets.

"Fine," Adam snapped. "Thirty minutes."

Dylan banged him on the upper arm as he left. "Looks like you got your wish, buddy."

Adam grunted.

"OKAY," ADAM SAID to Serena Long, feeling sweaty and unkempt in the presence of this woman who exuded control. She reminded him uncannily of a woman he'd once arrested. A renowned dominatrix who went by the name of Madame D. It didn't help that she was wearing all black— including boots. No doubt it was stylin', but he had the uncomfortable notion that what was in her briefcase— also black—might be a selection of leather-and-stud instruments.

"Okay?"

"Thirty minutes. I'm all yours."

"I was thinking—"

"Starbucks around the corner," he said. "Give me ten minutes to change."

She regarded him coolly, then nodded.

He headed for the change room, grabbed a fast shower, dragged a razor over his face and was back out, feeling a lot more in control, in fifteen minutes.

Serena Long was where he'd left her, more or less. She had a tablet computer on her lap, her cell phone wired to her head. When she saw him, she said into the mouthpiece, "I have a meeting with a client now. I have to go." Keeping her eyes on Adam's, she added, "I don't want to keep him waiting."

Ouch.

She put her gadgets away and rose. He followed her out the door. Even the way she walked reminded him of Madame D. That long, easy gait, the subtle sway of her hips. There'd been nothing outlandish about Madame D in her street clothes, either. She'd simply appeared to be a very sexy, beautiful woman. It wasn't until you got behind the facade that you got spanked.

He had no intention of letting that happen with this woman. Once a man let himself get vulnerable with her type, the next thing he knew she was using his cojones as dashboard ornaments.

He insisted on buying the coffees, which gave him a chance to check out the coffee shop as he did every public place. It was an instinct honed by years of policing. Nothing remotely suspicious seemed to be going on. Most of the clientele consisted of business types grabbing a java on the way to the office. A couple of joggers ahead of him ordered green tea. A few singles sat at tables with computers or newspapers in front of them.

When they were sitting down at a table that was too

small for him, as most café tables and chairs were, she said, "So are we going to keep fighting for control?"

Only years of training stopped him from choking on his coffee. How had she read his mind like this? Her cool gaze assessed him. He felt a pull of attraction so strong he could barely focus.

He swallowed the hot, bitter brew slowly. Instead of answering her directly, he said, "I don't think I need a performance coach."

"I've known Max for a decade. He's probably the smartest person I've ever met. And he's known you since you all played together in the sandbox. He seems to think you do."

"Max's trouble is he's always the smartest guy in the room. Makes him arrogant."

She let the words hang for a second, then said, "And your friend Dylan?"

His discomfort with this conversation grew by the second. He fidgeted in the too-small chair, ordered himself to relax. She must read body language as well as or better than he did. He put his elbows on the table. Leaned in. She leaned back slightly in response. Good. Her long hair caught the light and he realized it wasn't simply black, as he'd thought, but a shifting mix of brown and black. "I didn't play at the top of my game in the play-offs last year. It happens. Check out the NHL sometime. Best team going into the play-offs loses in the first round. Most expensive player on the team falls on his ass. Like I said, it happens."

"Your friends seem to think that you didn't simply have a bad couple of days in both of the last two play-off seasons. They think you choked."

He was getting more irritated by the second. He wondered how he'd managed to stay friends with such a pair of meddlers for the past three decades. "You should know that if you start putting ideas in a player's head about choking and performance anxiety, you're sowing the seeds for trouble."

"That's an interesting phrase you use. Performance anxiety. Do you think you suffer from it?"

"No. You're putting words in my mouth. I—"

"They were your words, Adam."

"Look, it's an amateur tournament. We raise money for charity. It's not the Stanley Cup."

"Then why are you getting so worked up about this? Maybe I can help you. Maybe I can't. The best thing that can happen is that I help you improve your playing ability during the play-off rounds. The worst thing that can happen is that nothing changes. Either way, my services are free and all you're giving up is some time."

"What about you? What's in this for you?"

Her fingernails were longer than strictly necessary. He had a momentary vision of her dragging them down his back in the height of passion. He had to blink the crazy mental image away.

"Max is a good friend who's done a lot to help me build my business. If he asks a favor, I'll do it. No questions asked."

It was stupid to feel a pang of jealousy. Max was a great guy and very successful with women. If he and the dominatrix performance coach had a past, it was nothing to do with him. Still, some devil prompted him to ask, "And Max? Would he do anything for you?"

Her gaze stayed level on his. "I like to think so."

He took another sip of coffee. "I don't know."

"It's up to you. If you're not willing to work with me, to do any exercises I give you, then we're both wasting our time."

"And if I do? If I promise to do your exercises and whatever else you ask of me? Can you guarantee my team will win Badges on Ice?"

When she laughed, her whole face lightened. She had even white teeth, a little wrinkle at the top of her nose that crinkled when she smiled. "If I had that kind of power, I think we'd be sitting here bartering for your soul. At least." She set her cup down. "Here's what I can guarantee. If you work with me, you'll know that your performance is the best it can be on that day. That you're not getting in your own way."

There was an uncomfortable ring of truth to those words. *Getting in your own way.* Did he do that?

"Give an example of one of these exercises."

"I'll give you one right now. And I want it completed next time we meet." She pulled a well-worn leather planner out of her bag. Interesting that for all her gadgets she still relied on paper. "I think we should get right on this. How's tomorrow at lunch for you? You can pick the place."

"Yeah. I can do that. What's the exercise?"

"I want you to go through the plays you messed up on last year's play-off game. In visual detail, and reimagine them as successful plays."

"I've played dozens of hockey games since last year. I can barely remember the championship game."

She drilled him with her eyes. "You remember every second of those games. And you've tortured yourself over and over again reliving your mistakes."

"I—"

"Don't. We both know the truth."

She was right, damn it, and the uncomfortable silence only confirmed her words. He'd spent sleepless nights going over every second of play, every moment when he should have been on top of his game, and instead he'd felt a big weight on his chest and a strange feeling of panic.

He didn't want to go back there and experience that panic again, not even in the privacy of his home. He wanted to get out there and prove he had the guts and skill to lead his team as he did all year long. To be a winner.

"I'll try," he said.

She shook her head. "Let's work on a different verb. Not try."

"Okay. I'll do it!"

"Good." She put her planner away and glanced at the slim gold watch on her wrist that was so expensive he bet a lover gave it to her. His mind sped to Max, who could afford to buy every watch, watchmaker and watch factory in Switzerland if he so desired. "Well, our thirty minutes are up. I'll see you tomorrow."

He rose as well, mostly because his mother would smack him on the back of the head if she caught him slouching while a woman was leaving.

She held out her hand and as he clasped it, he thought that her long fingers and those red-tipped nails would look just right wrapped around the handle of a whip. Uncomfortable heat coursed through him.

As she released her grip, she said, "By the way, what was your wish? The one Dylan said you got?"

He stared at her for a moment, debating with himself, then decided, what the hell. She'd asked. He leaned a little closer, the way he would if he were at a party wanting to get to know a woman better. "I told Max that if I had to work with a female performance coach, she'd better be hot."

She didn't sputter or blush or act coy. She said, "Well, it's nice to know your friend thinks I'm hot."

"Oh, he's not the only one."

3

WHEN SHE ARRIVED home at the end of a long day, Serena was so tired she wanted to throw a frozen dinner into the microwave, pour herself a huge glass of wine and flop on the couch.

But her blog waited.

She could hear her inner saboteur muttering, *I don't want to blog tonight. I'm too tired.*

Negative thinking, she reminded herself. Negative thinking got you exactly nowhere. Her success was the product of hard work as well as talent and she never let herself forget it. She was a big believer in the saying that success was 1 percent inspiration and 99 percent perspiration.

She updated her blog every Monday. In a perfect world she'd update more often, but she tried to use her time as wisely as possible and once a week was a reasonable compromise.

As was a glass of wine, she decided.

She unzipped her boots, put her clothes neatly away and dragged on her oldest, most comfortable pair of jeans and a favorite pink sweater.

Then she poured herself that glass of wine. Instead of the microwave dinner, she took the extra few minutes to put brown rice in the steamer and a chicken breast in the oven and throw together a salad.

She sipped her wine while dinner was cooking and settled herself in front of the computer. In forty minutes she'd have the blog post written and dinner would be ready. She could do this.

She pulled up her website. The woman staring back at her from her home page seemed to have all the answers, all the confidence in the world. She'd paid a professional photographer a lot of money to get that message of confidence across.

To hide the truth that deep inside she was desperately afraid that one day she'd be found out as the fraud she was. That she wasn't calm and confident. Inside she was the scared little girl who was hungry more often than not. Who collected cans and bottles off the side of the road in order to— *Stop it,* she ordered herself. She wasn't that helpless little girl anymore and she'd worked hard to become the woman she now was.

What would she even write about?

"Negative Thinking." The words were typed before she even realized she already had her topic for the week.

An image of the undeniably gorgeous, rough, tough hockey-playing detective—who was probably as much of a mess inside as she was—rose before her.

One thing you learned when you lived with secrets was that everyone had them.

What were Adam's secret insecurities? The ones that were keeping him from playing hockey to his full potential? He probably didn't even know. Neither, at this point, did she.

But they'd find them. He'd be a fun case, she decided. Once she got through his barrier of pride and toughness. There was a guy who didn't let people in easily.

She knew the type well. She was exactly like him.

He was also her weakness. There was a moment when the screen wavered in front of her eyes and she saw not a blank page but a very sexy image of a tall, rugged, ruthless man who took what he wanted without waiting for permission. She shivered, then shook off the ridiculous fantasy. Adam Shawnigan was a client, not a potential lover. She did not, she reminded herself, have time for a lover.

"Negative Thinking." The cursor blinked, inviting her to continue.

I know more people who have been brought down by negative thinking than by any other cause. How do you fight an enemy when the enemy is you?

Once she'd begun, the words poured out of her. Before she realized it, she'd written a longer blog post than usual. Her glass of wine was empty, the chicken was cooked and the rice was quietly staying warm for her.

She served herself dinner on the kind of china that she'd seen on TV shows when she was a child. The soap operas her mom loved to watch and her personal favorite, *The Fresh Prince of Bel-Air*. Watching that show, she'd first begun to realize a person born poor could have a different life. Even now she recognized that a lot of her work was about helping clients live a different life, creating the future they dreamed of.

Sure, she could eat off everyday plates, except that she didn't own any. When Serena Long ate dinner, she did so on fine china that she'd worked hard to afford. She drank out of crystal glasses and her cutlery was sterling.

While she ate, she checked the email account associated with her blog.

Often she gained new clients or opportunities to speak

through her website and blog. Her assistant monitored the emails regularly and passed on anything that needed answering, but Serena also checked in herself now and again.

She pulled up the current emails. There were three. Considering she hadn't given a speech recently or been mentioned in the media, three was pretty respectable.

The first was a thank-you from someone who had heard her speak and been inspired to face their fear of the water and enroll in beginner's swimming lessons. Serena experienced the familiar feeling of pleasure when she realized she'd helped someone. A complete stranger she'd never meet but whose life she'd improved, even if only a little bit.

With a smile, she sent a quick message that basically said, "Congratulations! Keep up the good work."

Then she clicked open the next message.

Hi gorgeous, the message began. I bet you could improve my performance. Want to try? Call me. With a hiss of annoyance, she deleted the message. The amazing thing about the perverts she heard from was how unimaginative they were. Couldn't they at least put a little effort into their crude attempts to shock her or connect with her or whatever they were trying to do?

"I DID NOT go behind your back," Max stated, putting down the heavy chair with a thunk. Adam had called both his supposed buddies to help him move the furniture out of his living room so he could refinish the floors. In truth, he hadn't planned to sand the floors for a couple of months, but he had a mad-on and experience told him that physical exertion mixed with concentration was the best combination for getting rid of the mad.

Besides, making his sandbox pals come move furniture gave him an opportunity to berate them at the same time as he got free labor out of them.

"You hired a performance coach without telling me."

"Technically, I didn't hire her. She's working for free. And I told you I was going to do it."

"You didn't tell me she was coming to hockey practice this morning." He scowled at the memory of how she'd blindsided him with her cool sexiness and that uncomfortable resemblance to Madame D. His skin prickled with the attraction he was determined to ignore. "I wasn't ready."

"Most people would be pretty happy to have a professional performance coach helping them improve their game."

He felt twitchy and irritable. Unlike himself. Usually if he had a problem, he understood its cause and dealt with the issue, but he'd never been in a position like this before, where he couldn't control his behavior on the ice. The fact that he didn't feel in control around the sexy Serena Long only compounded his frustration. "Why is she doing you this favor?"

"So that's what's got up your butt," Dylan commented, flopping onto the couch they were supposed to be moving.

Max gazed at Adam for a long moment. "What did she say?"

"She said she'd do anything for you."

Max looked inscrutable. But then, Max worked hard at looking inscrutable. "That was nice of her."

"You're not answering his question, dude," Dylan said from his sprawled position on the couch. "He wants to know if you've had sex with the woman he's got the hots for."

"Is that what you want to know?" Max seemed to find this whole thing highly amusing, which only aggravated Adam more.

"No." He grabbed his end of the couch and motioned

Dylan off it so he could lift the other end. "Okay, yes," he grunted as they hoisted the thing into the air.

"I didn't set you two up on a blind date. You're supposed to focus on improving your game. So why do you care?"

"I just want to know."

Max carefully placed his chair in the corner of the spare bedroom. Dylan and Adam humped the couch in after him and pushed it against the back wall. "I don't think I want to tell you."

Dylan swore. "There's a cold beer in the fridge with my name on it. I don't care who slept with who—I just want to get this stuff moved so I can relax."

They continued moving tables, the TV and a couple of lamps. When they were done, they had nowhere to sit but the old oak kitchen table Adam had refinished himself. He pulled out three cold ones, thumped them down on the table. Regarded Max, who wiped off the top of his bottle before he drank.

"What do you think?" he asked Dylan. "Did he?"

"Sleep with Serena Long? Hard to tell. He's doing his inscrutable thing. You're the detective. What do you think?"

"I think he's playing with me." He slumped into a chair and grabbed his own beer.

"Yeah," Dylan said. "Why would sexy Serena sleep with him, anyway? What's he got to offer a woman like that? A genius brain? Billions in the bank? Those big brown eyes?" Dylan shook his head. "She wouldn't touch him." He touched his bottle to Adam's in a toast. "Not that you care."

"I don't." He tipped the bottle against his lips and hoped the cool liquid would dampen his irritation.

"What are you using on the floors?" Dylan motioned

to the now-cleared fir floor. It was original to the old cottage Adam had bought the year before and was slowly fixing up. It was a simple place, rustic and solidly built on a couple of acres of land. He'd known the minute he'd seen the run-down home that this was the renovation project he'd been looking for.

Since it had been rented for years and then left empty for a half a year after that, the place was a little dilapidated. And full of mice. But the old fir floors he'd revealed when he ripped up the filthy threadbare brown shag rug would come back with some work. The walls needed only patching and paint. The kitchen he could live with for a while since he rarely cooked. His first project had been the bathroom, most of which he'd done himself, with the help of a professional plumber. He'd patched and painted all the walls before he moved in, and he lived with the scuffed, scarred flooring.

But now he had a mad-on, and Max had done nothing to dissipate it. The floors were going to be sanded. And hard.

"I'll rent a commercial sander. See how they come up, then decide. Might do a stain, might just slap on some Varathane to protect them."

Dylan nodded. He was also a handy type. Unlike Max, who hired everything out and was currently checking email on his smartphone while they talked flooring.

As they finished their beer, the talk veered to people they knew, hockey, the upcoming play-offs.

"That performance coach sure is hot," Dylan said, seemingly out of the blue. "She single?"

"As far as I know," Max said. "Why? Are you interested?"

"Hell, no. I'm interested in winning the bet. I figure you're both so competitive that if you two are going to fight over a woman, one of you will end up with her. Leaving me closer to winning the bet." He grinned. "All those seasons of watching *Survivor* are paying off." He raised his beer bottle in the air. "To the last bachelor standing. Me!"

Max still hadn't volunteered the information Adam wanted by the time the guys were leaving. As they headed out the door, Adam turned to Dylan. "Why are we still friends with this guy?" he asked.

Dylan regarded Max. "He's short and a weenie. Makes us look good."

4

AFTER HE WATCHED the news, Adam was too restless to turn in. He flipped on his computer to check his email. Nothing of much interest. Ever since his old buddy had arranged a performance coach for him, hints of his playoff panic had begun to return. Today, in the presence of the sexy coach, Adam had felt his discomfort like an itch.

On a whim, he did a Google search of Serena Long. Of course she had a website. He should have known she would. All slick and professional, the site looked and felt expensive. The woman staring at him from his screen also seemed slick and professional—and expensive—with that hint of danger he'd detected.

Dylan was right, of course. He did want Serena Long. He couldn't remember the last time a woman had struck him like that, like a walking fantasy.

Some effusive comments about how wonderful she was, written by people he'd actually heard of, peppered the main page of her site. She'd authored a book that you could click to and buy right from the front page, naturally. The click of another button would give you details on inviting her to be a keynote speaker at your next big event.

And then she offered words of wisdom on her blog.

He rolled his eyes. Who didn't have a blog these days?

He clicked through to it. And found a post dated today. "Negative Thinking."

It was what she'd been talking to him about earlier. And she'd posted only a couple of hours ago. He settled back and read what she'd written.

Apparently, negative thinking was bad. He shook his head, wondering why he was wasting his time with a woman who was going to spout the obvious, but continued to read. And realized quickly that she was imparting some truly good advice. This wasn't simply a "Rah, rah, you can do it!" post but an article that contained links to research on brain function and referenced B.F. Skinner and behavior modification. Good old B.F. He'd studied him in college. The man had conducted a lot of experiments involving pigeons, if he recalled correctly.

Behavior modification was all about rewards for the new behavior. Serena argued that weight-loss programs like Weight Watchers were based on building a new routine, like eating better, and receiving rewards in the form of encouragement at group meetings or online, rather than simply feeling bad about being fat. Made sense, he supposed. For him, going to the gym regularly meant he skated a little faster when he needed to or noticed a little more power and agility in his stick handling.

Her article went on to say that negative thinking and the self-destructive behavior that came out of it also had to have some kind of perceived reward or no one would engage in it.

His snort of disgust was loud in the quiet house.

He thought of the times he'd screwed up in the championship games and felt the familiar churn of self-disgust. What the hell had happened to him?

He'd choked. He could argue all he liked that it was

just fatigue, a flu bug, preoccupation with work. But he knew, and he was pretty sure the entire team knew, that his problem came from inside.

Did this crackpot performance coach seriously think he got a reward from humiliating himself and letting down his team?

He turned off the computer and went to bed. But sleep didn't come. What kind of reward could he possibly get for choking under pressure?

With a curse, he flipped on the bedside light, went to his spare-room office and grabbed a pad of paper and a pen and crawled back into bed.

She'd asked him to go through everything that had happened that day. He supposed now was as good a time as any.

If Serena Long could figure out how he was rewarded for choking, she was worth all the big bucks they weren't paying her.

He found himself looking forward to their next session. Not only because he wanted to be fixed but because he wanted to see her again. He'd never been the bondage and S-and-M type, but when he recalled the way that black-clad coolly sexy woman had looked at him, he began to understand the appeal.

SERENA CONSIDERED THE elliptical trainer at the gym one of her best friends. The machine was a time-efficient work-out, improving her cardio and her lower and upper body while at the same time allowing her to catch up on the day's news via a headset and inset TV monitor.

While she pedaled in endless ovals and pushed and pulled the handles, she absorbed the day's news. It was the usual mishmash of drama, despair, politics and business with a few cute human-interest stories thrown in.

The upcoming IPO for Marcus Lemming's company, Big Game, was mentioned. She suspected she was going to have to up her sessions with Marcus given the level of media interest. His was a classic geek-makes-good story of a quiet nerd with few social skills who'd parlayed an adolescence spent in his bedroom gaming into a terrific business. The trouble was that he hadn't had the time, skills or inclination in high school to do all the things most other boys do, like converse with girls, date, interact socially, play sports. It was easy to find the source of his problem and fairly easy to fix it.

Her tougher client seemed to be Adam, a guy who'd clearly misspent his teenage years to the hilt. He had the unconscious confidence of a man who was a high school jock, popular with both sexes, smart enough to get by but not freakishly intelligent. According to Max he was a terrific hockey player and a dedicated detective. Why would a man like that have performance anxiety?

Max had no idea. She suspected from her brief meeting with Adam that he didn't know, either. She wondered if he'd spend the time and effort required to work through his feelings about choking under pressure during the play-offs. And if he did the work, would he be self-aware enough to be able to diagnose his own ailment?

Frankly, she doubted it.

As her workout ticked toward the thirty-minute mark, her legs began to feel pleasantly tired. Another fifteen minutes of a strength-and-stretching routine designed for her by a personal trainer to provide the maximum workout in the minimum time, and she was done. Serena worked out every weekday at the gym and had her routine so well honed she could be showered, changed and heading to her office within an hour of entering the gym.

Since she arrived and left at approximately the same

time every day, she had a nodding acquaintance with a number of other prework clients. Today Stanley Wozniak, a quiet hospital worker who had a similar workout schedule, took the elliptical next to hers. She smiled at him and he blushed deeply. Which he did every morning. It was obvious that he had a crush on her. She only hoped that he was too shy ever to ask her out and embarrass them both.

She might spend only thirty minutes on the elliptical but she liked to give it her all. At the end of half an hour she was breathing hard and sweating so profusely her shirt clung to her. When she moved on to the free weights, her trainer, Tim Patterson, strolled by. He wore the standard uniform of black sweatpants and a black T-shirt advertising the gym, and he filled both out to mouthwatering perfection. Of course, he knew it. An Australian who'd originally come to the United States to work in a ski resort, he'd stayed and was one of the most popular trainers. "How ya goin', Serena?" he asked her.

"Hi, Tim. I'm fine."

He stopped, adjusted the line of her shoulders, and ran a hand down her spine in a professional, friendly manner. "Keep your back straight."

He watched her do a couple of reps and nodded. "Nice."

"Thanks." She took a private session with Tim every month so he could change up her routine. In the year they'd worked together, they'd formed an easy, friendly relationship. Often, as now, he'd keep an eye on her in between sessions.

He didn't move on immediately. After glancing right and left, he said, "I heard Stanley changed his shifts at the hospital so he could work out every day at the same time as you."

Stanley's little crush had never bothered her, but the

idea that he'd change shifts to spend more time sweating beside her was a little alarming.

She narrowed her eyes, letting the weights down easily at her sides. "Reliable source?"

Tim's blue eyes crinkled in his tanned face. It was as though he'd been in the sun for so much of his life that his face was permanently bronzed. "Pretty reliable. He told me himself."

She began her second set of lifts. "Why would he tell you that?"

"Because I asked him. That bloke's got a serious jones for you." They both glanced over at where Stan was wiping down his machine, which meant he'd soon follow her to the weight area. "He's a nice guy. You could do worse."

"I don't think his little crush is too serious," she grunted. "And why is the second set always so much harder than the first?"

"Because you're working a tired muscle. Keep it up. You're doing great." He adjusted her shoulders once more and then patted her back before moving on.

But he left her with a crease between her brows. Was Tim telling the truth? She suspected it might be time to casually mention to Stanley that she had a boyfriend. It was time to resurrect Fictitious Fanshaw.

Even if she had been attracted to Stanley, which she wasn't, her schedule was too full to take on a man. To conduct any kind of a full relationship, she'd have to give up something else. And it had been a long time since she'd met a man interesting enough to make her consider restructuring her routine. An image of Adam rose in her mind, all tough and rugged and gorgeous. She did not, she reminded herself sternly, have time for a man!

Nip the Stanley situation in the bud, she decided as she showered.

Consequently, when Stan emerged from the men's change room, she was in the foyer conducting a one-sided cell phone conversation. "Okay, darling," she said, nice and loud so Stanley wouldn't miss a word. "I'll pick up the wine. You pick up the steaks." She laughed softly. "Love you, too, Adam." She ended the call.

Adam? The name had popped out while having a pretend conversation with no one. Why, oh why, would she picture Adam when she imagined a lover?

Stan looked so sad as she waved to him on the way out that she felt rotten.

Well, she'd taken care of the Stan situation. Now she had to nip her own little crush in the bud. She worked with men all the time. CEOs of Fortune 500 companies, athletes who were household names, celebrities who suffered inexplicable stage fright. Sure, she'd experienced the odd thrill of being one-on-one with the rich, powerful and famous, but she never found herself fantasizing about them. Why should one rugged, uncooperative cop throw her off her stride?

She shook her head. It was going to have to stop.

When she arrived at her office, her assistant, Lisa, was already there. "What's the matter?" Lisa asked. "You look so serious."

"I was nipping buds."

The younger woman nodded. "Oh."

A psych major, Lisa had taken the job of Serena's personal assistant in order to gain job experience in the field of psychology. At twenty-three, Lisa was full of energy, keen to learn and packed with book knowledge that sometimes came in handy. Serena suspected she'd lose her PA in a couple of years, either so Lisa could pursue an advanced degree or so she could move to a more senior job, but for now the arrangement worked for both of them.

Her big blue eyes and Cupid's-bow mouth made her look as innocent as a milkmaid, but Lisa combined street smarts with school smarts. A scholarship student, she'd worked her butt off to get into college and to keep up her GPA while attending school and juggling part-time jobs. Nobody had more respect for the process than Serena, who'd done the same thing a decade earlier.

"Anything interesting happen yet?"

"Marcus Lemming asked to come in and see you. You had a slot at eleven, so I put him in for an hour."

She nodded. "Okay. I usually go to his office. I wonder why he's coming here."

"He didn't say. Also, I forwarded an email to you about speaking to an engineering company. I'm going through the rest of the mail now. I'll forward anything good."

"Great. I'll go check."

She took a couple of steps toward her office when Lisa's voice stopped her. "Oh—" Her voice sounded as if it had been cut off.

Serena turned. "What?"

"A creepy email."

"Oh, yeah. I thought I deleted that. It came last night." She shook her head. "You'd think perverts would have more imagination. Performance coaching. Ha, ha. I get it."

Lisa didn't smile. "This isn't one of those messages. It seems kind of threatening."

"What?" Serena didn't waste time going to her own computer and firing it up. Instead she stepped behind the reception desk and peered over Lisa's shoulder.

Interesting post tonight, Serena. Negative thinking. Think about this. You think you're better than fear? No one is. I can make you scared. I know you. I'm scaring you right now.

Watch your back, bitch. I will teach you what real fear is.

The message ended with a smiley-face emoticon, which, strangely, added to the nastiness.

5

SERENA STOOD THERE FROZEN, stuck in the moment as though she'd been superglued there.

She forced herself to step back from Lisa's computer. "Well, somebody's got a strange sense of humor."

"I don't think they're being funny," Lisa said. She rubbed her arms and Serena saw goose bumps there. "I don't like it."

"I'm not thrilled, either, but it's only somebody at a computer terminal sending an anonymous message."

"Have you pissed anybody off lately?"

She could think of only one person, but Adam Shawnigan was in law enforcement and definitely not the kind of guy to send creepy messages. He was up-front about his frustration.

"No. I don't have enemies. I specialize in positive thinking, improved self-image. I pump people up. Who would threaten me?"

"I think you should call the police."

"Why? Because some lonely weirdo tried to scare me? I won't give in to fear. I won't."

"Okay. But I'm keeping the email. If you get any more, I really think you should report the guy."

"So long as I ignore him, I'm sure there won't be any more."

She tried to put the email out of her mind, but the vague threat had lodged and didn't want to budge. She ignored her discomfort by getting busy with work. She called the engineering firm and accepted an invitation to speak at their yearly conference, which would be held in Chicago three months from now. Then she worked on a draft of the column she wrote for a business magazine every other month.

Even as she wrote about the importance of holding positive messages in one's mind, a very negative message whispered over and over: *I will teach you what real fear is.*

When Marcus Lemming arrived at eleven, she was staring out of the window, something she never did.

Irritated with herself for being unnerved by a childish prank, she forced herself to smile at Marcus and invite him to sit down at the round table she kept in her office for small meetings.

"What can I do for you?" she asked.

He didn't meet her gaze, keeping it on the computer bag he carried around with him the way a child would carry a beloved teddy bear.

"I need to talk to you about fear."

ADAM RAN AROUND his neighborhood.

He'd never been one to be cooped up in a gym. To him running on a treadmill was like trying to get somewhere in hell. He liked to feel the air on his skin, see what was going on around him. He often tried out different routes, so he had a pretty good sense of his neighborhood. He knew which roads had wide shoulders and thin traffic. He had learned which dogs always came out barking or sniffing and took a wide berth around the home of Rex, the Pomeranian who'd once taken a chunk out of his ankle.

As he pounded out the miles, he pondered. Cases under investigation, usually, but this morning he was thinking about hockey. About negative thinking. And how the hell the two got mixed up in his mind only during play-offs.

Didn't make sense.

He was a detective. Nothing drove him crazier than things that didn't make sense. He ended his run at a public park with an outdoor gym and dropped to the ground for a hundred push-ups and the same of abdominal crunches.

He was an early riser and finished his shower with a good half hour to spare before he was due at the office. So, as he did at least once a week, he dropped by his parents' place, which was on the way to work.

His dad had retired from the force at fifty-eight and now, in his early sixties, seemed to spend most of his time planning elaborate cross-country trips in an RV and doing community work. He was often at meetings of one community group or another.

When Adam arrived at the back door, his mom hugged him, as she always did. "I had a feeling you'd come," she said. "I baked muffins."

"You never bake muffins for me," Dennis complained.

"They're for you, too," she insisted.

Adam sometimes wondered if his mother had taken lessons from the TV since she was more like a screen mom than any of his friends' mothers. She baked from scratch, she sang to herself when she cleaned the house and she'd volunteered so much at school when he and his sister were growing up that he sometimes felt he'd seen her more than he'd seen some of his teachers.

Almost as amazing, she and Dennis had been happily married for almost forty years.

She put three muffins on his plate, poured him a mug of coffee exactly the way he liked it and placed the works on a floral place mat on the kitchen table, complete with a matching napkin. His father got only one muffin, but Adam didn't comment. He knew the diet his doctor and wife had forced on him was a sore point with his dad.

When they sat down, Adam's mom placed glasses of orange juice in front of both men.

"Roy Osgood decided to stay on as president of the local Rotary Club for another year," his dad said before biting into his muffin.

Adam got the feeling this was part of an ongoing discussion, guessed his dad had been interested in the post himself.

He watched as his mom ruffled her husband's hair fondly. "Not everyone can be president, honey. Besides, it's the worker bees who really contribute to an organization, much more than a man with a gavel."

"I know. I'm staying on the gardening committee. There's a lot to be done." He turned to Adam. "We're trying to get rid of invasive nonnative weeds in the public parks. It's amazing what damage those things can do."

"I know. My yard's full of them. Can't you make my place a community project?" he joked.

"You know I'll come anytime."

"Yeah. Truth is, I want to get the inside fixed up before I put much energy into the landscaping."

He ripped a muffin in half. It was steaming and full of good-for-you-looking grains and blueberries. Stuffed it in his mouth.

"I thought when you bought that house you might settle down," his mother said. "I could not believe it when I heard you and Max and Dylan make that stupid bet about the last man standing. Why don't you want to get married?"

"Because you've spoiled me. Where would I get a woman like you?" he said before stuffing the second half of the muffin into his mouth. He was only half joking.

"WHAT ABOUT FEAR?" Serena's voice was sharper than she'd intended and Marcus blinked at her.

"Remember? You said for some people fear of public speaking is worse than their fear of death. I think you even blogged about it."

Her hand drifted to her throat. "You read my blog?"

He stared at her the way she imagined he'd stare at his computer screen when a piece of programming didn't behave logically. "You suggested I read your blog."

She had to shake this foolishness. "Of course I did. I'm just surprised you found the time." She sat down, pulled out a pad of paper. "Okay," she said. "You want to talk about fear."

"Yes." He took a deep breath. "I develop games because that's what geeky kids with no friends do. Except I turned out to be really, really good at it. Now I'm worth millions and own a big company and most of the time I don't know what the hell I'm doing."

She nodded. This was familiar territory. She'd worked with athletes and musicians, people who suddenly found themselves famous, rich and with responsibilities they hadn't anticipated. They hadn't had the time or training to prepare themselves mentally or physically.

"Your whole life has changed," she told him. "Sometimes people feel as though they don't deserve their good fortune, so maybe they sabotage themselves."

"You mean like Trog in 'Third Circle'?"

He'd referenced his own game, which was good. Except that it was one of those violent point-and-shoot games, so clearly for the teenage-male market that she hadn't been able to play it after the second blasted and bleeding alien hit the ground groaning.

She took a wild guess. "In 'Third Circle' doesn't your hero have to perform certain tasks to get to the next level?"

"You mean like vanquishing death meteors?"

"Exactly like vanquishing death meteors. Why don't you work on that? Imagine that your fear of public speaking is your death meteor. How are you going to extinguish it and move to the next stage? Remember, you're the hero of your own game."

He was nodding, looking not enthusiastic exactly but more engaged than he had been last time she'd seen him.

"I could do that. I think."

"Okay." She saw that noon was fast approaching and she had a meeting with Adam at twelve-thirty. It didn't matter to her that he was a pro bono client and Marcus was paying big bucks. She didn't make schedule changes if she could help it. She rose. "All right. I think we've had a bit of a breakthrough. Why don't we schedule you another session right here in my office? Maybe it's good for you to get away from your own building for a while."

He nodded. "Okay."

She walked him out to the front. Lisa glanced up from her computer, quickly removing her glasses.

"Marcus needs another appointment. Can you schedule it?"

"Yes, of course."

Lisa glanced up at Marcus. "I have to tell you, I really love 'Third Circle.'"

Marcus dropped his gaze immediately to his computer case and mumbled, "Cool."

"When's 'Third Circle: Zombie Apocalypse' coming out?"

Marcus looked up from his computer case the most

animated Serena had ever seen him. "It's going to be so rad. We're working out a couple of kinks. Can't get the zombie blood right. I mean, what color is zombie blood?"

"Do zombies have blood?"

"Excellent question."

Serena could not believe two intelligent, educated adults were having a conversation about the color of zombie blood. But it gave her an idea.

When the two paused in the midst of their geekfest, she said, "Marcus, why don't you try reading your speech to Lisa?"

"What, now?"

She'd meant at a later appointment and was about to say so when Lisa said, "Sure. That'd be sweet. Unless you have somewhere you have to be."

"No," Marcus replied. "I do most of my work at night." He shrugged. "Habit of a lifetime. I'd like to read it to you."

"Awesome."

"Okay," Serena said. "I'll be back in the office at two."

"Sure," said Lisa, not even glancing her way. "See you then."

As she was leaving the office, she heard Lisa say, "If there really was a zombie apocalypse, where would you hide?"

"No, see, that's a mistake a lot of people make. You can't hide. You have to run."

ADAM WAS WAITING at the restaurant when she got there. She'd let him choose the venue and he opted for a Mexican restaurant. "Sorry," she said when she arrived a couple of minutes late. "I got caught up in the zombie apocalypse."

Her client looked more relaxed than he had the last time she'd seen him, in well-worn jeans that showed the powerful muscles in his thighs and a navy sweater.

"Huh?" he said.

"Do you have opinions on whether it's better to run or hide during the zombie apocalypse?"

He blinked at her. "Have you been drinking?"

She smiled. "Thank you, Adam. I feel so much better." She settled at the table. He'd taken a seat with his back to the wall and she saw him scan the crowd, no doubt looking for lawbreakers or potential trouble. She doubted he even noticed he was doing it. The decor was typical. Tiled floor, rustic wooden tables, sombreros and Mexican kitsch on the walls. Mariachi music played, but softly, so you could hear yourself think. "What's good here?"

"Everything. I like the enchiladas myself."

She nodded, scanned the menu rapidly. Chose a taco salad. As soon as she closed her menu, a waitress appeared and they gave their orders. A basket of tortilla chips and salsa arrived almost immediately, with the iced teas they had both ordered.

"So? Did you do your homework?"

"Yes, teacher. I did my homework."

She felt a smile pull at her lips. She was relieved he'd dropped the attitude. He'd clearly made his peace with working with her, which gave them much better odds of figuring out the root of his problem.

"Good. Did you discover anything interesting?"

"You don't waste time, do you?"

"Not if I can help it. The sooner you have your issues under control, the sooner you can live up to your full potential."

"Do you really believe that?" he asked as though he really wanted to know.

"Yes. Of course I do. It's what my entire career is based on."

Those blue, blue eyes of his made her forget this was

a lunch meeting and imagine, almost wish, it were a romantic get-together. A date. The kind where you bolt your food because you're so anxious to get home and get naked. "Maybe some people aren't meant to do great things."

She bet he could do great things in bed, then was shocked to realize that her thoughts were taking a whole different path than their conversation.

"Of course they aren't. So long as you feel you are living the life you want, that you aren't getting in your own way, I have no quarrel. I know people doing menial work at minimum wage who are happier than you or I will ever be. They find real satisfaction in what they do. They are living up to their potential. In your case, with the Hunter Hurricanes, you play at peak performance all year until the play-offs and then your game suddenly deteriorates. Why? That's what we want to work on."

"It was weird. I started writing out the games like you told me to and I got this feeling, like guilt, that came over me. It got hard to breathe and I had trouble staying in my chair to write it all out."

He reached for a wad of folded paper in his pocket but she stopped him. "Tell me about it."

"Well, I remember last year's championship pretty clearly. Game was tied 2–2. And frankly, they never should have got two goals. Our defense was sloppy—mostly, though, our offense was weak. So I'm open. I yell. Dylan shoots me the puck. I've got a clear shot at goal. I mean, you could have nailed the shot. No offense."

"None taken. What happened?"

"The game was won. It was over. A little tap of my stick on the puck and the cup was ours."

"And?"

She heard a sound that might have been his teeth grinding together. "I missed the puck."

"Wow."

"Yeah. I shot and missed the damn puck. A three-year-old with a plastic stick could have got that puck in the net."

"Interesting." She sat back and thought about what he'd told her. "What do you think you felt guilty about?"

"I don't know. It's like I wasn't supposed to win the game."

"You weren't supposed to win the game," she parroted. "According to whom?"

"Hell if I know."

"Who has the power to make you play at less than your best?"

"I do!" The words exploded from him. She felt his frustration and imagined writing out the games had been a difficult exercise.

"Of course you do. But someone or something else is sending you messages. I want you to think about that. Go through your day and really listen. Whose standards are you trying to live up to? A coach's? A teacher's? A parent's? A boss's? Some kind of authority figure, probably from your childhood, has buried these land mines in your subconscious. It's up to you to find them and disarm them before they do any more damage."

"What am I listening for?"

"When have you heard these messages before? You can go back to childhood and listen to the past. Replay conversations you can remember, particularly if they were around winning and success. See what comes up for you."

"How will I know when I find it?"

She loved how focused he was, how he gave her every scintilla of his attention. She had another momentary flash of being naked with him and shivered. Found her own focus—on the damned topic at hand.

"I remember working with a woman once who could

not communicate anger. She was the worst doormat you've ever seen. Everyone in her life took advantage of her and she let them. It was making her ill. Actually ill. She got migraines and more colds and flu bugs than anyone I'd ever met. When she did this exercise, she started hearing her mother's voice saying, 'Good girls never show their temper.' When she was young, if she yelled, she was punished. So she learned never to show her anger. Always to show a smiling face to the world and do whatever anyone asked of her. Once she recognized that she'd taken those messages inside and gone completely overboard, she was able to work on expressing her feelings."

"Wow." He looked genuinely impressed.

"There's a kind of resonance when you see the pattern. An 'aha' moment. Chills down the back of your neck. You'll know it when you experience it."

She watched him polish off the last of the largest plate of enchiladas she'd ever seen.

"What was it for you?" he asked when he'd swallowed. "Your 'aha' moment."

She smiled at him. "One day I'll tell you. But today we're focusing on you."

"One day I hope you'll tell me a lot of things." His voice was warm, intimate. She felt the pull of attraction so strongly she knew she was lost.

There was a beat of silence. Their gazes stayed locked. Then she forced herself to pull them back to the reason for their lunch. "Why do you play hockey?" she asked him.

He looked at her as though this were some kind of test question. "Because it's fun."

"Good. That's excellent. That's exactly why you should play a game. What do you like best about it?"

He reached for the basket of tortilla chips and chose one. "I like the game itself. Strategy, when a play works, scoring a goal, but most of all I like the camaraderie. After a game we'll have a beer in the dressing room and talk about stuff. Joke around." He put the chip in his mouth. Crunched down.

"Male bonding."

"Yeah."

He chomped more chips. She got the feeling that if he'd known her better, he'd have reached for the half of her salad that she hadn't been able to finish.

"All right. Here's your homework for next week."

"Will it give me writer's cramp?"

"No. I want you to listen for those messages we were talking about earlier. If you can find the source, then we're going to be close to improving your performance."

"Okay." He scooped the last three chips out of the basket, swooped them through the remains of the salsa.

"And I'm going to give you a couple of mantras."

"Couple of what?" A bright red drop of sauce sploshed on the table as he halted the chips a couple of inches from his mouth.

"Mantras. Affirmations. Statements you repeat many times throughout the day, especially right before you play. She pulled a notebook and pen from her bag. Spoke aloud as she wrote.

"First one—it's okay to win. Second—I am allowed to win. Third—hockey is fun. I love it and don't take it, or myself, too seriously."

"Oh, the guys are going to love hearing me mutter that crap before every game."

"You can repeat it silently." She watched him fiddle with the ceramic donkey salt and pepper shakers. "Adam." She waited until he met her gaze. "You have to trust me."

"I do or we wouldn't be here." His eyes continued to stare into hers and she felt warmth kindle in her belly.

She saw his desire for her, felt her own reflected. To her consternation, she dropped her gaze first. "Good," she said briskly.

When they emerged into the parking lot, he walked her to her car. It was kind of sweet and old-fashioned and she loved it.

As soon as she'd unlocked her car, he opened the door for her. She glanced up. "Thanks." Found him far closer than she'd imagined he'd be. So close she could see the stubble forming on his skin, the intense expression in his eyes.

"Serena," he said.

"Yes?"

"I've had an 'aha' moment."

"Really? What is it?"

"I don't think this is going to be a strictly-business relationship." Before she could respond, he'd closed the tiny distance between them, pulled her to him and closed his mouth on hers. Hot, determined, possessive, his lips covered hers. He gave her a moment to accept or reject his caress and she used that moment to angle her body closer, to open her lips in mute invitation.

He took her mouth then, licking into her, giving her a taste of his power and hunger. Which, naturally, incited her own. And, oh, she was hungry. He reminded her of how long it had been since she'd lost herself in a man.

A tiny sound came out of her throat, half moan, half purr. He took that as encouragement and pulled her even closer, kissing her deeply and thoroughly. She felt his arousal as he held her tight against his body, felt her own arousal blast through her.

A car with all the windows open blasting music roared into the parking lot and he quickly pulled away, shielding her with his body.

"Aha," he said.

She gazed up at him, stunned at the strength of her own response. "I don't date my clients," she reminded them both.

"I don't recall asking you for a date," he said, all sexy and pleased with himself.

"You're going to be trouble, aren't you?"

"Oh, I hope so."

She still had the shivers down the back of her neck as she got into her car and drove away.

6

ADAM COULDN'T REMEMBER the last time a kiss had knocked his socks off like that. That woman was something, he decided, as he thought about the previous day. He'd have her in his bed sooner rather than later. He was already enjoying the anticipation.

His partner, Joey Sorento, wasn't sharing Adam's good mood. In fact, Joey seemed to grow more pessimistic with each passing day. He had a dream of moving back to his family's ancient vineyard on Sicily where Sorentos had been making some of the best extra-virgin olive oil in the world for centuries. But he needed money to buy the place from his aging grandparents. He watched the stock markets the way fishermen watch the weather. Based on observation, Adam didn't think his partner was much of a stock picker.

Despite being a Sicilian, Joey didn't have the vaguest connection to the Mob. Didn't matter. He was known around the precinct as Joey the Virgin. Most everyone called him Virge.

They'd been sent out to investigate a suspicious death in a leafy neighborhood in one of the more expensive suburbs of Hunter.

"Who called it in?" Adam asked as they drove.

"Neighbor. She went in to water plants. The guy was supposed to be in Hawaii for the winter but when she went in this morning, she found him dead."

Pretty much any time someone died at home, their death was deemed suspicious, except in cases of terminal illness. Most of these calls turned out to be natural deaths— heart attacks, strokes, choking. Or suicides. When they arrived at 271 Greenleaf Road, everything seemed calm. They entered through a gate, walked up a brick path and before they'd reached the front door, a woman appeared behind them. "I'm Vera Swann. From next door," she said. She was in her sixties. A prosperous-looking woman. She seemed a little shaken. "I thought Norman was in Hawaii. I went in to water his plants, like I always do when he's away." She put her hand to her heart. "And I found him. I'm sure he's dead. I used to be a nurse. I called 911. You beat the ambulance."

"Can you let us in?" Virge asked.

"Yes, of course."

The house was modern in design but smelled musty and sort of damp. As if it had been shut up for a while. Vera Swann led them into a den/TV room and there was Norman, still in his bathrobe. A newspaper was open on his lap and his head was tilted forward.

Adam approached, checking the area as he did so. Nothing suspicious. He checked the guy's pulse. The skin was already cold and waxen. He nodded. "Dead."

"Looks like a jammer," Virge said.

"Yep. Or a stroke."

"Coroner will figure it out, I guess."

Because they were there, they followed protocol and did a quick walk-through of the house. Adam checked out the upstairs, and Virge took the basement.

While he was wandering through empty bedrooms wondering where he and Virge should stop for coffee, he heard a yell. Virge didn't get excited by much, so the yell sent him pounding down the stairs, through the main floor and down to the basement.

"Well, well, lookie here," he said as Virge walked among rows and rows of constructed wooden planters sporting thousands of leafy green plants. "We've got ourselves a grow op."

SERENA REALLY LIKED it when her speaking engagements were in Seattle. Oh, she'd travel wherever the work took her, but it was so nice to drive to the conference center or a big hotel, give a workshop or luncheon address or whatever was asked of her and head home to her own bed. The Pacific Northwest Executives Association was today's client and they'd booked her for most of the day. They'd hired her to present a breakfast address called "Reaching for Success" and later a workshop on inspiring optimal performance from employees.

Between the two, she had a quick meeting with the owner of a chain of salons and spas about giving an all-day workshop to the company's staff and contractors. It was more work and Serena was grateful to be so in demand, but she needed to clone herself.

As soon as the afternoon workshop ended, she hopped on the I-5 and headed not for home, as she would have liked, but to meet Adam at her office.

She was tired, feeling a little scattered. She could cancel, but she didn't. She liked Adam. After his initial resistance she felt that he'd come on board and was willing to do the work required to solve his problem. He was also very nice to look at.

She returned to the office at four-thirty. Adam was

coming at five, which gave her time to return calls and take care of any pressing business. "Hi," Lisa said when she walked in. "How did it go?"

"Great. I think the workshops went well and we likely got some more business because of it."

"I like your new suit. The blue suits you."

"Thanks. First time I've worn it." She didn't tell Lisa that she had a personal shopper at Nordstrom who called her when new stock came in in her size and style. The woman knew Serena's wardrobe almost as well as Serena did. Serena didn't like wasting time shopping but she needed to project an image of professionalism and sophistication. She had to appear to have it all together even when that felt laughably untrue. However, having her own shopper made her feel vaguely guilty and self-indulgent, so she tended not to mention it.

While she quickly flipped through the messages Lisa handed her, she paused at one. "Marcus was in today?" She glanced at Lisa. "We didn't expect him, did we?"

"No." Her assistant held her gaze but her color rose. "I…um…I want to talk to you about something."

"Okay." Now wasn't the time. She was tired and Adam was on his way, but instinct told her she needed to listen to Lisa. And do it now.

"What's up?"

Lisa fiddled with her hair, a sign she was nervous. "I love working with you. I enjoy the clients and I can see that you really make a difference in people's lives."

Sure, Serena thought, *butter me up. Then stick it to me.* She merely nodded and waited.

Lisa stacked the Post-it notes beside her computer, then straightened a perfectly perpendicular pen. "I see that you have to turn down work, that you have more clients than one person can possibly handle." She licked her lips. "I want to take on more responsibility. Maybe one day become a junior partner." The last part came out in a rush, as though she'd memorized the words but hadn't practiced the speech enough times.

Serena felt one more weight added to her already overburdened shoulders. She'd known she'd lose Lisa; she simply hadn't expected it to be this soon. "I work alone, Lisa. I always have. I admit I'm a control freak. I can't imagine having a partner. I think I'd always be double-checking your work to make sure it was done the way I'd do it."

"But you could train me. I'm a fast learner."

"When would I have time to train you? I've barely got time to eat lunch."

"I really feel like I could be an asset. Marcus came in today because he asked me to go over the last exercise you gave him. I was able to explain things to him when you were busy with something else."

A spurt of irritation blasted through her. What right did Lisa have to explain her exercises to a client? The woman was her admin assistant, not a certified performance coach.

Before she did something stupid like say things she might regret, Serena said, "Can you let me think about this for a few days? Maybe we can talk again after I've had time to digest?"

"Yes, of course."

As Serena was heading to her office, Lisa said, "I followed your advice, you know. You always say if you don't ask, you won't get."

She turned.

As Lisa was speaking, the outer door opened and Adam walked in, flashing his killer smile at the pair of them. "Ladies." If his eyes telegraphed wicked messages, they were only for her.

Perfect timing, Serena thought as she welcomed him, glad he'd broken into a conversation she didn't want to finish. "Come on back to my office."

When she looked at him, she forgot Lisa. All she could think about was that kiss, that earthshaking, spine-melting kiss that she'd thought about far too often in the past few days.

She wanted him, she realized, looking at the long-limbed, sexy man with the killer blue eyes.

Since he'd never been here before, she watched him take in her decor, neutral and modern. He flicked a glance at the original abstract painting on her wall, another at the Dale Chihuly sculpture centered on the glass-and-cement table in the center of her office. Then he sank into one of the pair of black leather Eames chairs.

She did a little checking out of her own. He'd had his hair cut recently, she noted. It was crisper around the edges and a little shorter than last time she'd seen him. A nice thick head of hair that would feel good beneath her fingers the next time she found herself in his arms.

Oh, stop it.

Before she could open her mouth, he said, "So what did I walk in on?"

"I beg your pardon?"

"You and your gal out front were looking pretty tense when I walked in."

"It's nothing. Now, did you—"

"Seems you spend a lot of time delving into my head but have damn thick walls around your own psyche."

"It's supposed to be that way. You're the client."

"Max calls it a favor for a friend. I'm offering you the same favor."

"But we're not friends," she snapped without thinking.

It was as though she'd played right into his hands. A

slow smile began to form. "If I'm not your client, and we're not friends, I wonder what we are."

The moment that followed was so loaded with sexual heat Serena was amazed her new suit didn't melt right off her body, leaving nothing behind but a few blue threads clinging to her skin like slivers of heaven.

Perhaps because she didn't feel like dealing with their obvious sexual attraction, or maybe because she really needed somebody to talk to and he was the closest ear, she said, "If you really want to know, Lisa, who is the best assistant I've ever had, wants to become a junior partner. But I've never had a partner. I work alone. I can't imagine having to train someone, to monitor their progress, to…"

"Trust them?" he said softly.

"I trust Lisa. I do," she insisted when he lifted a quizzical eyebrow. "It's just that I can't imagine sharing clients and—"

"Giving up total control?"

"Maybe." She sighed. "Probably."

"Do you have enough work to add another person?"

"I'm swamped. I'm turning down work."

"Do you trust her?"

"As much as I trust anyone."

"Aha."

"Stop with the *ahas*. This is your session."

"But I made you think, didn't I?"

He was so pleased with himself she had to smile. "Yes. You did."

"She got the chops? Professionally?"

Serena nodded. "She's got an MA in psychology. She's good with people. She reminds me of myself at her age. Without the baggage."

He flicked her a glance that suggested one day soon he

was going to be asking about her baggage. She wondered what she'd do when that happened.

"What happens if you don't give her more responsibility?"

She sighed. "I'll lose her to somebody who will give her a better chance."

He leaned back, opened his hands palms up. "Something to think about."

"You're right. Thanks. Now let's turn to you."

"Okay. I had a good week. Even though they make me gag, I recite those affirmations about twenty times a day. Scored more goals in Tuesday's game than I've scored in a single game all year."

"Congratulations."

"So I figure I'm cured and you look hungry. How about I take you out for dinner somewhere and we can pick up where we left off in the parking lot."

Oh, he was smooth. And seductive. And she wanted to walk away from the office and her problems and let him take her to dinner and then home to bed more than she wanted to admit. But she'd taken on the job of coaching him and she was determined to see it through.

"Not so fast." She leaned back. "You've never had a problem in regular play. It's the play-off games where you have your issues. I don't think you should celebrate too soon."

He seemed pretty unsurprised by her reaction and only rolled his eyes before saying, "I haven't figured out the part about where I get the guilt from."

There was a moment's silence. She said, "Tell me why you became a cop."

He shrugged. "I don't know. I always knew I was going to be a cop. Ever since I was a little kid. My dad was a cop, of course, and a good one. He was the hero in our house. Seemed natural to go the same route."

"Lots of people have parents they admire and they don't go into the same line of work. Give me another reason."

She watched him thinking, casting back to earlier decisions he probably didn't remember making. She gave him the time he needed. Finally, he said, "This is going to sound stupid."

"Good. We're getting somewhere."

From the way he appeared a little sheepish she suspected he'd tapped into memories he'd nearly forgotten. "When I was in elementary school, I was walking home one day and there was a group of older kids. They were bullying some kid who was a bit of a misfit. You could tell he'd peed his pants and they were tormenting him." He glanced up at her. "Do you really want to hear this?"

"Oh, I really do."

"It was stupid and reckless. I walked up to them and told them to knock it off. Me against probably five or six older guys." He scratched his nose. "I was always big for my age, but they were bigger. And I was definitely outnumbered."

"What made you do it? What was the impulse?"

He looked at her as though he weren't really seeing her. He was looking back into his past.

"It was the right thing to do," he said finally. Simply.

Urge to protect. A strong sense of justice. Not the worst reasons to become a law officer. "What happened?"

"I got into a fight. I got beat up a little. Would have ended a lot worse if Dylan and Max hadn't come by." He grinned at the memory. "Those guys didn't stand a chance."

"Do you still feel like you're fighting injustice?"

"Working in policing, I often feel like I'm fighting big

battles I can't win. The bad guys have the money—they can afford resources we can't. They kill witnesses. It's a tough job. Getting tougher all the time." He settled back into his seat. "But we do what we can. Catch enough bad guys that I can sleep at night."

"You make the world a safer place."

"One tiny corner of it. At least, I try."

"Do you think—"

The text message alert went off on her smartphone, interrupting her.

"Oh, I'm so sorry," she said. "I forgot to turn off my phone." She was annoyed with herself and with Lisa. If her assistant hadn't picked such a bad moment to have their little talk, Serena would never have been so unprofessional as to forget to turn off her cell.

"No problem."

She reached for her phone to switch it off, but the words of the text were right there. She read the message and a garbled sound came out of her throat. Part scream, part moan.

Adam crossed the room in a stride. "Serena, what is it?"

He squatted in front of her. Took her wrists in his hands.

She couldn't seem to form words. She simply handed him the phone.

You should wear blue more often. Makes a nice change from all that black. Your heart is pounding with fear right now. I'm so close to you. I can feel it.

The text ended with a smiley-face emoticon.

"What the…?" Adam squeezed her wrists gently where a pulse beat crazily. "Serena? Who sent this? What's going on?"

"I don't know." Her voice didn't sound like hers. It

sounded like the scared little girl she hadn't been for a long time. "I don't know."

"How long have you been getting these messages?"

Adam had his cop face on, she noted. Hard eyes. Watchful expression. The hands gripping her wrists felt strong. Capable.

"This is the first time he's texted me. How did he get my number?"

"I don't know. You say this is the first time he's texted you? So there have been other messages?"

She nodded, trying to pull her thoughts together. "Yes. Some emails. I thought they were pranks. I get inappropriate emails through my website. It happens. But these were creepier. Threatening." She shivered.

"Did you keep them?"

She nodded. "Not me. I won't have that negative garbage in my space. Lisa kept them on the office computer."

"Good. Can you show me?"

"Lisa—" She glanced at her watch. "Damn. Lisa's gone for the day."

"We can get her back if we need to. See if you can find them for me."

"Yes. Of course. I'm being stupid. Sorry."

"You're doing great," he said soothingly. He rose and held out his hand. She clutched it, letting him pull her to her feet. Even now she wondered if there was a camera recording her. Microphones. How had some nutbar invaded her space like this? He knew what she was wearing? Today was the first day she'd worn that blue suit. She felt watched. She felt violated. Vulnerable.

Why would someone want to scare her?

The why was bad enough, but the part of her inner questions that really disturbed her was that there was also a who. A faceless, anonymous creep who wanted to scare her.

Which brought her right back to *why?*

7

She led Adam out to the main office. Lisa had left the reception area immaculate, as she always did. Serena booted up the computer.

It took her a couple of minutes of searching but she found the file Lisa had insisted on making containing the disturbing emails she'd received.

"Here it is." She clicked open the file. Adam leaned over her shoulder. She felt ridiculously reassured by his big strong capable presence.

"This was the first one?" He clicked on the message amd frowned.

"Yes. I've been getting one every few days. As you can see, they all basically say the same thing. I don't even read them. If Lisa gets to them first, she puts them in the file so I don't have to see them. If I get the message first, I forward it to her."

He read them all in order. Didn't comment until he got to the end. "This is all of them?"

"Yes."

"Have you told the cops?"

"No."

"Why not?"

"Because it's exactly what he wants me to do, act scared. I refuse to give some negative fearmonger the satisfaction."

"This guy could be a dangerous psychopath. He didn't get any reaction from the emails. Now he's upped the ante. Shown you he's capable of getting closer to you. That he's watching you. You need to go to the cops."

"Maybe the text and the emails are from different people," she said.

He shook his head. "I don't think so. They all talk about fear. And every one of them ends with the same emoticon."

She ran a hand through her hair, lifted it off the nape of her neck and let it drop again. "I won't give in to fear."

He laid a hand on her shoulder. "Fear isn't all bad. It can be a healthy response to a danger that's very real."

"You're not helping."

"Serena, you need to take this seriously." He squeezed her shoulder, then said, "Let's leave it for now. I'll walk you to your car."

"All right. Let me lock up."

He watched her routine, turning off the computers, then the lights. To lock her office she punched a code into an electronic panel.

As they walked down the hallway to the elevators, she was embarrassingly glad to have Adam beside her. She didn't want to be a victim, but right now she felt too vulnerable to be alone. How had her creepy email guy known what she was wearing?

The possibilities made her nervous.

She was a bit surprised when Adam didn't walk her to her car and leave her. He said, "I have a better idea. I'm going to take you for dinner. You need to eat and I need to ask you some questions."

"No." She knew she sounded panicky. "I don't want to go out in public. Not right now."

"Okay. I'll take you to my place. It's completely safe. No one would think to look for you there."

His place. Safety. Also a chance to see how he lived, what was important to him. Because whatever else he was right now, he was her client and she still planned to help him face his demons.

But…his place.

He looked at her and suddenly grinned, as though reading her mind. "You'd be giving up control. Not easy for you to do." His expression turned serious. "And you'd be trusting me." He moved closer. "You can, you know."

"I don't think you're a psychotic texter, if that's what you mean."

"It's not what I mean and you know it."

She nodded. A wave of fatigue struck her. She was tired. She'd been going nonstop for so long, days as packed as today, and the murky discomfort of those emails had always been at the back of her mind. Now the person sending them had stepped things up and she felt as though she needed a little break from it all. A chance to breathe and refocus, find her balance.

Of course, Adam knocked her off balance in a completely different way. But she did trust him. And she really didn't want to go home to her apartment and wonder if some kook had cameras trained on her or something.

"Can you cook?" she asked.

"Depends. If you like spaghetti, bacon and eggs, or steak on the barbecue, then yes, I can cook. I also do great takeout."

"All right." She turned to him. "And thanks."

"We'll figure this out. You're not alone. Come on."

"But my car…"

"I'll bring you back for it. I don't want you driving out in it until I know more."

Serena reminded herself that he was the cop. There was no point arguing with him about what he did best. She wasn't stupid. She knew that the person sending her those threatening emails had taken a huge step today, letting her know he could see her. Assuming it was even a he. She knew nothing about this person and the feeling of helplessness was infuriating.

Adam drove a nondescript sedan that didn't quite scream cop but strongly suggested civil servant. As they drove, he kept the conversation light. Told her a fairly amusing story about his last hockey practice. She felt herself relax a little and was grateful to him for this small respite.

When they reached his house, she was surprised and delighted to see an old-fashioned cottage on a large piece of property. The garden cried out for attention. She mentally painted in an assortment of flowers. Nothing too formal—it wouldn't suit the cottage—but maybe a rosebush in that corner and some wildflowers in the meadow. She could see where a vegetable garden had once grown and it was easy to picture it bursting with fresh herbs and a crop of homegrown veggies. Five or six apple and cherry trees bravely hung on. She wondered idly if they could be saved.

"What a great place," she said.

"Thanks. I bought it last year. It's a work in progress."

The driveway was new and smooth as he pulled in and parked near the front entrance. Two steps led up to a freshly painted white porch with a purple clematis vine curling around the wooden pillars and overhang. If it were hers, she'd put window boxes under the multipaned windows on either side of the porch.

"Come on in," he said, unlocking the blue front door, which was also freshly painted.

"Thanks."

She stopped inside to look around.

"Like I said, a work in progress."

"With so much potential."

She loved it immediately. The old-fashioned kitchen with its cheerfully painted yellow cupboards, the scarred wooden counters. The living area featured heavy-beamed ceilings painted white to match the walls. The floors gleamed with history. "I love the floor," she said, bending to get a better view. "Original?"

"Oh, yeah. Fir. I refinished them. It's my most recent project."

She could see the scars and pits that decades of footsteps and items dropped and dragged had left there. She loved that he hadn't replaced them with brand-new floors. Or torn out the kitchen to go with granite and stainless. He'd kept to the original idea of a cottage. Simple and functional. A river-rock fireplace in the main living room wall was already set; all that was left to do was light a match.

She liked the efficiency of her own gas fireplace, which flickered to life whenever she pushed a switch on the wall, and she enjoyed her sleek granite and stainless kitchen, so efficient and modern. She knew how much more work a place like this would be, but it had a homey feeling that her own apartment somehow lacked.

A short hallway off the living room must lead to bedrooms and a bathroom.

His furniture was obviously chosen for comfort over style. Big oversize couch, a leather chair with an ottoman that faced a big-screen TV.

"Sit down," he said, ushering her into the living room.

She sat on the couch, sinking back into the cushions, which seemed to hug her into themselves. He went to the fridge. "I've got beer or some wine."

"What kind of wine?"

"I don't know. Somebody gave it to me for my birthday." He read the label. "It's a chardonnay from California."

"That would be fine, thank you."

He brought her a glass of wine and himself a beer, then settled himself in the leather chair that was clearly his favorite spot.

She sipped her wine, feeling suddenly nervous now that she knew the small talk and the house tour were over. He had his cop face on.

"So," he said, "tell me what's been going on."

"I told you. I've been getting somewhat disturbing emails. You read them."

"And you're a smart woman. You've had a few weeks to think about who your enemies are, who might be jealous of you or want to hurt you."

"I really didn't think too much about them at first. I'm a fairly high-profile person with a public website. I get emails from people who are maybe very lonely or a little crazy or from perverts who think it's highly amusing to misunderstand the meaning of *performance coach*."

He made a wry face but remained silent.

"I was going to delete them. I try not to keep anything negative in my personal space." She felt the effort he was putting into not rolling his eyes. "But Lisa made me keep them. She's the one who's been filing them, as I told you."

"Good for Lisa."

"It wasn't until that text today that I realized it has to be someone who knows me. Who could see what I'm wearing."

"Tell me about your enemies."

"I don't have any."

"I hate to be the voice of doom, but I think you do."

She took another sip of wine. "Nobody obvious springs to mind."

"Okay. A jealous rival? As you say, you're pretty high profile. Have you pissed off another performance coach? Is there someone out there who thinks they deserve all your success?"

"Of course there are other coaches who aren't as successful, but it's like that in any business. I'm sure there are people who would love to have my career, but they can. Anyone can be successful if they put some effort into it."

He held up a hand. "Okay. Don't want your coaching philosophy—I want you to think of people who might be jealous enough that they'd try to hurt you."

"I can't think of anyone."

"What about Lisa?"

"Lisa? My assistant?"

He nodded. "She wants to be a partner. And you don't take partners. Maybe she's pissed enough to try and take you down. Remember, that text came right after I walked in on a kind of tense moment. Maybe she decided to rattle your cage."

"But we work together. I've mentored her. I trust her."

"Not enough to bring her into the business."

"That's different."

"Maybe it isn't to Lisa."

She couldn't stand the thought of Lisa sabotaging her. "Lisa is the one who made me keep the emails. She's keeping the file. And—" she hated to admit this "—Lisa suggested I tell the police. I'm sure she's not behind this."

She doubted he was as certain, but he didn't pursue Lisa anymore. "Okay. Personal life. Lovers."

She felt a warmth tinge her cheeks. "I don't have any lovers." Or much of a personal life, if she was honest.

"Former lovers. Old boyfriends with a grudge."

"I try to leave every relationship on a positive note."

He stared at her for a long moment. "I can't help you if you spout bullshit off your website. Or out of your self-help book."

8

SERENA RUBBED HER forehead with the heel of her hand. He might think she was lying when she said she tried to leave relationships in a positive way but it was true. She wouldn't be successful if she didn't believe what she wrote and practice what she preached.

But somewhere along the line, somebody had developed a serious grudge against her. And Adam was a detective trying to help her. She thought back to her longest relationship. Tried to sum it up.

"My longest relationship was with Carl. He's a theoretical physicist. We never lived in the same city but got together on a regular basis. When it was clear he was more interested in proving the existence of the Higgs boson particle than he was in me, we parted." She smiled. "He was one of the team of scientists who proved its existence. Exciting stuff. He married another physicist. Last I heard, they were living in Geneva. I don't think he'd wish me ill."

"You're right. Sounds unlikely to be Carl Higgs Boson. Who else?"

"I—" She hadn't realized how lacking her love life had been. In the three years since she and Carl had split, she'd barely dated. Looking back, it was clear that she and Carl had stayed together for years because both had other passions. They both put their work first. Sporadic companionship, a date for their big events, mediocre sex. It had been enough. For a while.

Since then? She shrugged. "I've dated, but nothing serious."

"What about Max?" His voice held a hint of urgency that would have been easy to miss.

"Max? Max Varo?"

He nodded, leaning forward, his beer held loosely in one fist.

"Max and I have been friends and colleagues since we did our MBA together. He's always had a string of completely unsuitable women and we never felt that way about each other."

"Good." As Adam settled back, it occurred to her that he was relieved she and Max had never been an item. And his reasons had nothing to do with her new email pal.

"Also, I don't think he's the type to send creepy emails."

"We'll take him off the list, then."

"I dated a basketball player I coached. Not until after he worked through his issues, of course. I never date my clients."

Their gazes connected and she felt the sizzle of attraction, the challenge of trying to deny it.

"What happened there?"

"It was great for a few months but..." She looked back on her time with Mike. He'd been full of energy, inventive and insatiable sexually, but in the end... "I think we ran out of things to talk about."

"You're still friends?"

Were they? "I don't think we're enemies. But I can't say we really stayed in touch. I wish him well. He's dating a supermodel now."

"How long ago was this?"

She thought back. "About a year…no, eighteen months ago." Had it really been that long? She'd become so focused on work that she hadn't really paid attention to her lack of a personal life.

He didn't say anything to that, merely frowned. "Well, somebody wants to hu—scare you, anyway. In my experience it's usually someone you know."

She tried not to shiver but it was awful feeling as though it could be someone she knew, talked to, maybe saw on a regular basis, did business with, coached— She gave a small gasp.

Naturally, Mr. Detective immediately picked up on it. "What?"

"No. It's ridiculous."

"How 'bout you tell me anyway?"

"I coach this young internet entrepreneur. Usually I go to his place of business, but right after I got the first message, he changed the pattern. He's been coming to my office. The first time he came by he said he wanted to talk to me about fear. Naturally, my first thought was that he'd sent the email, but it turned out he was talking about his fear. He's a little inept socially. I'd forgotten all about it. I'm sure he'd never—"

"Socially reclusive. Knows the internet well enough that he could send untraceable emails. Shows up at your office? Sounds like we have a possible winner."

"How do you know those emails are untraceable?"

"I don't. It's a hunch. We detectives are famous for them, you know." His eyes crinkled a little around the edges and she knew he was trying to make her feel better.

Wasn't working.

"I'd like to have a little talk with this guy."

"And scare away one of my top clients? I don't think so."

"He could be threatening you."

"Why? Why would he?"

"Why do crazy people do things?" He threw up his hands. "I don't know. Maybe the stress of his sudden success is curdling his milk. He sees a beautiful, sexy woman like you and knows he could never have her. There could be all kinds of crazy in his head."

She had to stop focusing on the fact that he'd called her beautiful and sexy. She had to concentrate on the troubling messages. But there was a sort of jumpy excitement in her belly that reminded her she was sitting across from the most sexually exciting man she'd met in ages.

Now they were alone in his house. And she really, really wanted to get naked with him.

"I don't want you talking to my client. He sees me in my office. My assistant is always there." She tried to imagine Marcus Lemming sending her threats and simply couldn't. "You know, I'm a pretty good judge of character and I've never had any sense of something being off with Ma—my client."

He leaned forward. Pinned her with an intense blue stare. "Listen to interviews with the neighbors and coworkers of a serial killer sometime. Mostly they can't believe that such a nice young man could do such awful things."

Since there was no point in arguing about whether Marcus Lemming might be a serial killer, she took refuge in her wine. The glass was nearly empty and in spite of the conversation topic she was starting to feel more settled.

"You hungry?" he asked.

Surprisingly, she was. "Yes."

"Pizza okay?"

"That would be perfect."

He stood up. "I'll call it in." He strode past her and paused. "You're not going to make me get some weird-ass pizza, are you? Duck and seaweed or something?"

She chuckled at his tone of horror. "No. I'm happy with something traditional."

"Excellent." He lifted the receiver on his landline and hit a number on speed dial. She guessed he ate a lot of pizza. "Pepperoni, mushroom and green pepper. Pizza as God intended it."

"Extra cheese?" she asked.

He grinned at her. "You might just be the perfect woman." Then he was speaking to the pizza place and she was spared an answer. Which was a good thing because she couldn't think of one. Perfect woman? She was an emotional mess who preached balance to her coaching clients but was so out of balance herself she hadn't had a relationship in a year and a half and had barely noticed. Worse, she was so clueless that she had an enemy she hadn't known about.

Adam put down the phone. Told her the delivery would be about twenty minutes, then remained by the phone frowning. "If you won't let me open a case file on this, then I'm going to need two things."

This sounded very much like bargaining. She didn't feel like bargaining. "What?"

"First, you let me show the emails to a colleague of mine. A profiler. She's a friend. She'll keep my request confidential if I ask her to."

She thought about it. Realized the request was reasonable. "Okay. And the second thing?"

"We bring Max in on this. You know that one of the companies he owns is a top security firm, right?"

"Yes." Max loved planes and flying and space, and he owned a regional airline. But he was also a smart entrepreneur. He owned media outlets, a couple of online businesses and a big security company that was one of the best in the country.

"But—"

"I want your apartment and your workplace scoured for bugs, hidden cameras, any kind of surveillance equipment."

The text had mentioned her blue suit. The possibility that someone had somehow installed a camera in her apartment without her knowledge was extremely unsettling. She put a hand to her stomach. He was right. If there was something there, she wanted it out.

"All right."

"Then we put in our own equipment."

Her eyes went wide. "But—"

"It's for your protection."

"The text mentioned my blue suit. So what? A few hundred people saw me wearing it today. You're jumping to conclusions."

"Putting safety first."

She looked into those eyes that had seen things she didn't even want to imagine. Which made him a lot more knowledgeable about criminals than she ever wanted to be. "Okay."

He called Max. Told him Serena was with him and that they wanted to talk to him. She didn't hear what Max said, but it was a pretty short conversation. Sounded as if one of the busiest men she knew was dropping everything at an old friend's request.

The pizza arrived. Adam poured her a second glass of wine and tore off squares of paper towel for napkins. They settled across from each other at the round oak table in his kitchen.

While they pulled pieces of pizza out of the box, so

stringy with extra cheese that they had to tear at it with their fingers, he said, "I would have pegged you for the brown-rice-and-tofu type."

"Some days I am," she admitted. "But I believe a little indulgence every once in a while is good for a person. Don't you?" When she glanced up at him, she saw such a blaze of sexual heat in his eyes that a tremor of lust shivered across her skin.

"Oh, I believe a person should indulge. Yes, indeed."

She hadn't meant her words to be interpreted that way and he must have known it. But she also realized there was little point in denying the obvious. They were hot for each other. As inconvenient and poorly timed as this crazy attraction was, it was as real as the pizza they were devouring.

He waited until she'd eaten her fill and as he polished off another slice, he said, "Let's go through your day. Every second of it from the time you got up this morning."

She'd known this was coming, of course. He was a cop. Questioning the victim. Her jaw tightened. If there was one thing she refused to be, it was a victim.

"I got up at six-thirty, as I do every morning. I prepared and ate a yogurt smoothie. Then I threw on my exercise clothes, picked up the suit bag I'd organized the night before and drove to my gym. I arrived a few minutes before seven. I put my things in my locker in the ladies' change area. I worked out on the elliptical for thirty minutes, then did some mat work. Then I showered, dried my hair, did my makeup and dressed for the day."

"In the blue suit?"

"Yes."

"How often do you go to the gym?"

"Every weekday unless I'm sick or out of town."

"Same time?"

"Yes."

"You work out with the same people?"

"Quite often."

"Who saw you after you were dressed and on your way out?"

"I don't know. Fifty people."

"Any that you know by name?"

"I know some of the women. We chat in the change room."

"Write down their names."

"What?"

"Tonight. Before you forget who you saw this morning." He saw that she was about to argue. "You don't have to show me the list. Keep it in case. Who else did you see?"

"There are always staff coming and going from the front area. Trainers, cleaners, sales people. A few people I recognize but never talk to. My trainer, Tim, spotted me for a few minutes while I lifted weights. A man I see there often came by to say that he'd given my book to all of the staff in his company because he'd read it and enjoyed it so much. That was nice."

She sighed.

He obviously picked up on the distress behind the sigh. "What?"

"Stanley." She knew she had to tell him about Stanley.

"Who's Stanley?"

"Another gym client. He works out on the machine next to mine in the gym. He's an X-ray technician, I think. He has a little crush on me." She felt miserably guilty talking about poor Stan like this.

"How little?"

"Maybe not so little." She couldn't imagine the polite little man who blushed every time he saw her sending those strange, hurtful messages. But then, she couldn't imagine anyone in her life doing such a thing.

"How long has this crush of his been going on?"

"A few months."

"Did anything happen around the time you first started getting the emails?"

She nodded. On some level she must have wondered about Stanley from the beginning.

"Tim told me Stanley had changed his shift at the hospital so he could work out at the same time as me every day. I'd known he had a little crush on me, of course, but when I knew he'd changed his work schedule to work out with me, I decided to let Stanley know I wasn't available. I didn't want him embarrassing both of us by asking me out. So I waited until he was in earshot and had a fake conversation on my cell phone with a supposed lover." She blushed slightly remembering that she'd uttered Adam's name during that call. "I got the first email soon after."

Adam's face went hard. "Stanley have a last name?"

She hesitated.

"Serena, what he's doing is harassment. I'll check him out discreetly."

"Wozniak."

He didn't make notes. He must have quite a memory.

"Did Stanley say anything to you this morning?"

She felt like a worm. "He said, 'You look very pretty today, Serena,' and then he held the door open for me. I thanked him, got into my car and drove away."

There was a beat of silence. "Then what did you do?"

"I stopped in at the office briefly and then I drove to the conference center. I gave a breakfast speech to about two hundred executives and then later on I gave a smaller workshop. There were fifty or sixty people in the room."

"You know any of them?"

"Probably a dozen quite well. Others well enough to exchange pleasantries. I had coffee with the CEO of a chain of salons and spas who's interested in having me speak to her employees. Then I drove back to the office."

"Did anyone come into the office while you were there?"

"Lisa. You."

"Is there someone you can stay with tonight? I don't want you going back to your apartment until Max has it checked out."

"You're being paranoid. I have to go home."

"How about for one night you don't?" He was so serious she decided to stop arguing. She didn't really believe that there were cameras hidden in or around her apartment. But the possibility was awful.

"I can go to a hotel."

"No family?"

"No."

"Friends?"

Friends who'd offer her a guest room? She had a few, she supposed, but what would she say? "I'll be fine in a hotel."

"Why don't you stay here? I've got a spare room. I even have a spare toothbrush."

Before she could answer, the kitchen door was simultaneously knocked on and opened.

Max walked in, followed by their firefighting friend Dylan. Both men wore running shorts, athletic shirts and sneakers.

"We were jogging when you called," Max said. He jerked his head in Dylan's direction. "He insisted on riding along."

Dylan had already discovered the pizza box and flipped it open and was tearing into a slice with big white teeth.

"Thought you might need another hand," he said with his mouth full.

Serena couldn't think of a friend to call who'd give her a bed, and these guys dropped everything for each other. She wondered what it would be like to have friends you'd known forever, to have grown up in the same leafy suburb, gone to school together, got drunk together, had each other's backs. She didn't envy many things, but she found herself yearning for close-knit friendships like Adam's.

Adam glanced at her. "Okay if we let Dylan in on what's going on? He doesn't look like much, but you can trust him."

She smiled, as he'd meant her to. Nodded. "All right."

Briefly he related her story. If the other two men were shocked, they gave no sign of it. Max's jaw tightened and Dylan's hands fisted when Adam revealed the contents of the latest text message, but otherwise they simply listened.

When Adam was done, Max turned to her. "Are you okay?"

"Yeah."

"Good. I'll get you a bodyguard. The guys we hire are the best. Most of them ex-military or ex-cops."

"A bodyguard? For a few weird emails? I—"

Adam interrupted. "Let's start with having your security company sweep her apartment and office for any surveillance equipment."

Max nodded. "I'll have a team there tomorrow."

"Discreetly. We don't want the perp to know we're onto him."

"Please. Do I look like a novice?"

Dylan, now on his second slice of purloined pizza, said, "Do you have anyone who can trace the emails and the call?"

"I'll do that," Max said.

"What can I do?" Dylan asked.

"Stand by."

He nodded. Ripped off a piece of paper towel and wiped his mouth. Turned to her. "These guys may act like the Keystone Kops, but luckily they're a lot smarter than they look. You're in good hands."

"Thanks."

Max turned to go. "I'll get the team set up for tomorrow." He looked almost apologetic as he turned to her. "I'll need keys, codes."

"Of course." She went for her purse.

"We'll do your office early. Before anyone gets in. I'll have a report to you as soon as I can."

She nodded. "Thanks."

"The apartment is easier in regular daytime hours. You okay with that?"

"Yes, of course."

"You have a place to stay tonight?"

"She's staying here," Adam said.

He and Max exchanged a look that clearly meant something to them and simply looked like an intense if fleeting glance to her. Then Max nodded. Headed for the door, Dylan in his wake. Dylan waved and headed out first. Max turned back. "Take care of her," he said softly.

AFTER THE OTHER two left, she was suddenly and deeply aware that she was alone with Adam, who had kissed her senseless in the parking lot of a Mexican restaurant. But that was before the text message. He turned to her. For a moment they were both frozen. What was the protocol here? She had no idea. Didn't seem as if he did, either.

"I'll get you that toothbrush," he said.

"Okay."

It wasn't that late. Barely ten o'clock, but she was bone

tired, she realized, from a long busy day followed by the
stress and emotional torment of those messages and the
way Adam and Max had reacted. As though she was in
real danger.

She busied herself putting the pizza box in the recy-
cling bin, tidying up, wiping the table.

When he returned, he had a toothbrush in its packet, a
small tube of toothpaste and a gray T-shirt that was larger
than some dresses she'd owned.

She accepted the offerings. "Thank you."

There was an awkward moment when she wasn't sure if
he was going to move closer or back away. She was rooted
to the spot, unsure which way she wanted the evening to
go. It lasted only a second and then he was turning away.
"The guest room's through here. It's not fancy but you'll
be safe," he said.

"Safe sounds good."

He must have heard the weariness in her voice. He
threw an arm around her shoulders, like a brother or a pal,
and squeezed. "We'll get this thing figured out. Okay?"

She turned to smile at him, found his gorgeous, sexy
male-model mouth kissably close to her own and resolutely pulled away. "Yeah."

"I sleep with my door open," he said. "In case you need
anything in the night."

They looked at each other for a long moment. She knew
it was up to her to move her lips closer, to be the one to
make the first move. But she was too strung out to make
any kind of an intelligent decision, so she tamped down
the lust roaring through her system. "Thanks," she said in
a voice so husky it barely sounded like her own.

As she crawled under the covers in the guest room bed,

she was surprised at how safe she felt. For now, at least, she could let go of the stress and tension knowing Adam was there. He wouldn't let anything bad happen to her.

9

SERENA HADN'T HAD one of the old nightmares for years. A little therapy, a lot of self-talk, some books on the subject had all helped her face the personal demons she still carried from her past. And although they had not healed completely, at least she was able to acknowledge her wounds until they scarred neatly.

So it was beyond awful to wake with the explosive fear pounding through her body, her heart banging and her breath caught in her throat. Some shadowy figure was out to get her and as she ran and ran, her steps grew slower. Couldn't catch her breath. Heard the dark, faceless man's pounding steps behind her, gaining. Gaining. She tried to scream and nothing came out. There was something bad ahead, a dark place, a big yawning cave mouth, and because he was after her, she had nowhere else to go. Terror behind, terror ahead.

She whimpered in the dark. Her fear was so intense she felt dizzy.

For a panicked second she didn't know where she was. Strange shadows, wrong room. Then she pulled herself fully awake, remembered she was in Adam's guest room and why. She sat up and flipped on a light.

She'd never get back to sleep, not while adrenaline was careening around her system. She knew the minute she plunged the room back in darkness, the irrational fear would start up again.

Sitting up, she pulled her knees to her chest, reminded herself that she was safe. She waited until her breathing was back to normal and her heart was beating at a more reasonable pace.

She'd read. Reading always helped.

Of course she didn't have a book with her. She'd assumed she'd go home at the end of the day as usual.

The oversize gray T-shirt hung down to her thighs as she climbed out of bed and padded across the scarred wood floors. Easing the door quietly open, she entered the living room. She remembered seeing a bookcase stuffed with enough reading material that she assumed she'd find something that appealed. And if she discovered a book that bored her into slumber, so much the better.

Adam had mentioned he slept with his bedroom door open and she didn't want to wake him, so she resisted the impulse to flip on a light. Instead she used the dim beam from her smartphone to scan the shelves. She could make out a range of hardbacks, paperbacks, a couple of stacks of magazines, but she was having trouble making out the individual titles. She edged closer. Stubbed her bare toe on the foot of the big couch. Cursed silently.

As she leaned closer, holding her phone within inches of the book spines, she realized her host had pretty eclectic tastes in reading material. Sci-fi and fantasy, thriller, hockey biographies and history books.

She was torn between a book about the Russian Revolution and a biography of Bobby Orr when she saw a hardcover book entitled *Secrets of Sleep*. Perfect. She reached for it and her hand closed on the hardcover just as the overhead light flipped on and she jumped at least a mile into the air.

She turned, clutching the book to her heart, and saw Adam standing outside his door as alert as though it were midmorning and he were on his third cup of coffee. Only the low-slung boxer shorts and the messy hair gave away that he'd been sleeping. In the split second it took him to put his right hand behind his back she saw the glint of dark metal and realized he was holding a firearm.

"I'm sorry," she said. "I was looking for something to read." She glanced at the phone in her hand. "I didn't want to wake you."

"Can't sleep?"

She shook her head. "Nightmare." Why hadn't she stayed in bed like a normal person and waited for morning? "I'm sorry I woke you." She should have gone to that hotel. Maybe would have if she'd had her car with her. What a truly awful houseguest she was.

"You didn't."

"You were awake?"

He shrugged. Rubbed his chest with the knuckles of his left hand. She couldn't help but follow the movement with her gaze. The man had a spectacular body. Big, muscular, with biceps that made her think he could carry her tucked under his arm if he wanted to. His chest was broad, furred with dark hair that arrowed down, leading her eye south across well-defined abs to where it disappeared beneath the waistband of his faded navy boxers. He had nice legs, she noted, and big working-man feet.

She was ashamed of herself for checking him out like that. Then when she glanced at him, she realized he was doing some checking out of his own. All of a sudden she was keenly aware of the fact that she was naked but for his

T-shirt. Their gazes connected and once again she felt the pull of lust, as inconvenient as it was undeniable.

"Do you want some tea?" he asked when the silence had dragged a second too long and her heart had begun to thud.

"Tea?"

His chin was shadowed with stubble. His eyes had the sleepy, sexy expression of a man on his way to bed, planning to take her with him. "Yeah, tea."

"A second ago you were pointing a gun at me, now you're offering me tea?"

"Safety first. I heard somebody creeping around in here. Didn't know it was you."

And suddenly she realized. He hadn't been sleeping because he was on watch. It hadn't really occurred to her that whoever had written her that threatening text could have followed her here. She'd felt so safe. Now she shivered. "Thank you for protecting me."

"It's what they pay me for. Part of the service you get when you pay your taxes."

She had to smile. He wasn't on duty and she very much doubted that many citizens of Hunter got to stay in a police officer's home at the slightest hint of danger. "What kind of tea?"

"Sleepytime." He walked, barefoot, to the kitchen, opened a cupboard. "Or chamomile." He pulled a couple of boxes of tea from the cupboard, then grabbed a bottle of pills and placed it beside them on the counter. "These are herbal sleeping pills. Don't work as well as the real ones, but they help."

She held a book in her hand about sleep. He had a cupboard full of herbal sleep aids. He was wide-awake at 3:00 a.m. It wasn't difficult to come to an obvious conclusion. "You're an insomniac."

He set the kettle on to boil. "Only at night."

She chuckled. Picked up the herbal-remedy bottle. Listened to the rattle of pills. Put it down.

She opened cupboards until she found big blue earthenware mugs. Pulled two off the shelf. There was something ridiculously domestic about making tea at three in the morning in a man's kitchen, both of you dressed in next to nothing. Her skin felt super sensitized. When she reached for the mugs, she felt the soft cotton of his shirt graze her nipples, and even without turning, she was intensely aware of the big sexy presence behind her.

She turned to reach for the tea bags at the same moment he did. Their hands touched. A tiny shock of electricity zapped through her. She didn't look up. Couldn't. She moved away—all the way out of the kitchen—and settled herself on the couch at a safe distance. Thought about going to her bedroom and putting on…what? Her suit?

Don't make a big deal out of it, she told herself, and pulled the hem of the shirt down as far as it would go, then settled back on the couch, her legs primly together. Then she opened the book about sleep.

The kettle boiled, its whistle loud in the silent cottage, and as he padded over to her with the two steaming mugs of tea in his hands, she shut the book and placed it on the table.

"Thanks," she said, accepting the tea.

He nodded and sat beside her on the couch. She sipped her drink. Suspected it wouldn't help her get back to sleep, but the tea was hot and soothing, so she sipped again.

"Do you think whoever sent the message yesterday could have followed me here?" She didn't like even thinking it, but ever since she'd seen him all steely eyed and dangerous wielding that gun, she'd known the possibility existed.

"Maybe, but I don't think so."

She sipped more tea. It was oddly companionable sitting there with him.

"I haven't had a nightmare in a long time. I used to get them frequently until I worked with a therapist who suggested I practice something called active imagination."

He glanced at her over the rim of his mug and she got the feeling that she'd lost him somewhere between *therapist* and *active imagination.*

"The idea is that you go back into the dream once you're awake and confront the dark figure that's chasing you."

"Does it work?"

"Between that and a few other techniques, I was able to overcome the nightmares. Now I only get them in times of acute stress."

"Did you try it tonight? The active imagination thing? Maybe your unconscious knows who's sending you that crap. Maybe it's trying to tell you."

Okay, so maybe therapy and active imagination weren't so foreign to him after all. Interesting. "I wondered the same thing. I did try. But when I turned around, there was no one there. The footsteps faded as though the person following me had run away."

"Your subconscious is telling you he's a coward. Which, given the way he's been communicating, is not a big breakthrough."

They drank more tea.

"Do you suffer from nightmares?" she asked.

"Sometimes." The word was short and sharp. Clearly he didn't want to talk about his demons. "It's pretty common in my line of work."

She nodded. "Dreaming is one way we deal with trauma, how we sort out troubles and emotions."

"Why did you need therapy for nightmares?" he asked.

Normally she was as protective of her private life as

he was, but there was something about sitting here on his couch with very little clothing on, knowing he had her back, that made her feel like sharing. If nothing else, perhaps her candor would help him open up about his own issues.

"I had a very insecure childhood," she said at last. It was so quiet here. With no traffic sounds, it felt as though they were the only two people awake in the whole world.

"Your parents got divorced?"

She made a sound that was somewhere between a chuckle and a snort. "That was the least of it and happened when I was so young I barely remember anything but the fighting. No. Truth is my mom never should have had a kid. She wasn't suited for it. She wasn't much more than a child herself and had addiction issues."

"Oh, no." From the tone of his voice she suspected she wouldn't have to paint him any pictures of her life.

"Yeah. We were dirt-poor. I seriously think she only kept me because she needed the extra welfare money. I was hungry more than not. And she used to go out at night and leave me alone in the trailer."

He pulled her in close and she let him. Somehow the nightmare tonight and the feelings of vulnerability she'd experienced were bringing back the old fears. "I was so scared." She heard her voice start to rise and fought to bring it back down. "I'd beg her not to go out every night before I went to bed and she'd promise. But she almost always went out anyway. So I'd wake up all alone and frightened."

"That sucks," he said.

"Once, I was so scared I ran to the neighbor's. When she found me there, she took me home and beat me. She'd never hit me before. She said if I ever did that again, the cops would drag me away and make me live with bad people."

"You were powerless."

She nodded. "She wasn't a terrible person, but the drugs and alcohol made her pretty useless. By the time I was twelve I was running the place. Then things got a little better."

"How did you get from there to here?" He sounded amazed. "I deal with people who live that life. It's brutally hard to break the cycle."

"I've thought about that a lot. Strangely, I think TV saved me."

"TV?"

"Sure. No matter how poor we were, we always had TV. The only bonding my mother and I ever did was over television shows. She loved the big splashy soaps about all those rich folks. She'd say to me, 'When I get some money together, we're going to get a house. And buy clothes like Linda Evans and get a maid.'" Serena shrugged. "Of course I knew that was never going to happen, but what those shows taught me was that there was another life out there being lived by people who had enough to eat and didn't live in utter squalor."

"You've got some guts. That's a long journey from there to here."

"Well, the great thing about being a kid is you don't know how badly the deck is stacked against you." She sipped her rapidly cooling tea. "I don't think I would have got out if I hadn't had a couple of mentors in my life. Apart from the TV ones. There was a teacher at school. You have to realize that at my school there weren't a lot of college-track types. But I was smart and hardworking. I liked school. There were rules, order. I got fed lunch. And I had a teacher, Mrs. Brand, who told me about the scholarships that were available to people like me."

She stretched back. His arm was still around her and she liked the warm feel. Found she even liked telling Adam her pathetic childhood story.

"The worst part was I had to keep it all a secret. If my mom found out there was money coming my way, well, let's say it wouldn't have gone in my college fund. Everything went through Mrs. Brand. But I did it. I got into college with a full scholarship. I worked a couple of part-time jobs and studied my butt off. One good thing about my background was that I was used to living on nothing. I ate a lot of beans and rice. Bought my few clothes at the thrift store. And I watched how the other kids did things. Dumb little things you take for granted when you have a normal family. How they ate, how they dressed, even their table manners. I studied them and copied them."

"Did you make friends with them?"

His tone suggested he already knew the answer to that. She turned to look at him. "You're a perceptive guy."

"Detective. Remember?"

"No. I was an outsider. Plus, I was so busy working and studying I didn't have time for friends. I had a great boss, though. Another mentor. Ed owned the bakery I worked in mornings before school and on the weekends. We were allowed to take home day-old bread and things that didn't turn out for whatever reason. I lived on misshapen buns and cookies that were overcooked. I didn't care. After where I'd been? It was heaven."

"How did Ed mentor you?"

"He was from Poland. He'd come from a poor family and he knew all about hardship. He was a self-made man. And, as he liked to remind me, when he'd started, he didn't even know English. He had several businesses. I guess he was a little bit like Max. Anyhow, he was an amateur investor, a pretty good one. He taught me about the markets and he instilled in me the idea of being an entrepreneur."

She smiled in memory. "He was a wonderful man. He had a sweet wife and three kids he swore were turning into American brats. But he loved those kids like crazy. After I finished my business degree, I went to work for him on the corporate side for a couple of years. I built a pretty decent nest egg between saving a ton of what I earned and investing. But I was ambitious. As I'm sure you know, some of the greatest success stories in business are people who came from poverty. You get so determined never, ever to end up where you started that it's easy to become a workaholic.

"I guess those TV shows had really planted themselves in my brain. I learned everything I could from Ed and then I left to do my MBA."

"No hard feelings?"

Was Mr. Detective wondering if her old boss liked smiley faces? "No," she said firmly. "In fact, if I phoned him tomorrow and asked for a job, he'd give me one. We still have lunch once in a while. He gives me investment advice and now I'm able to offer useful suggestions about human-resources issues in exchange. It works."

"That's an amazing story. I had no idea. Figured you for somebody who came from money."

She smiled. "I learned everything, from manners to how to dress, act and talk, from TV and watching people. Especially people I admired. You know, we learn more than we realize from our parents. I had to consciously model myself on other people."

"You ever see your mom?" he asked gently.

"No. She died some years back." She didn't feel like talking about the mess of emotions she suspected she'd never really sort out where her mother was concerned and he seemed to understand.

"You have a real toughness about you. Now I see where it comes from."

"You have a real toughness, too."

"Comes with the job."

"So? How about you? Deep dark secrets? Family drama?"

"Compared to you? I grew up on the set of *Leave It to Beaver*. Weirdly, I sometimes think that's true. I mean, my mother bakes. Like constantly. She cooks a real dinner every single night. Roast on Sundays. Who does that?"

"And your father?"

"Also a cop. And obviously the reason I went into law enforcement."

"You see? It's what I said earlier. We either follow our parents' patterns and the attitudes we've unconsciously accepted or we go the other way. You and I chose exactly the opposite paths from each other. Quite dramatic, really."

"I guess." He turned to her. "Do you want more tea?"

"No, thank you."

"You feeling sleepy yet?" he asked her.

"No."

"Want to watch some TV?"

She wasn't remotely sleepy and neither, it seemed, was he. "Sure."

He flipped the remote and his big-screen sprang to life. "There's not much on this time of night, but we can watch a pay-per-view."

"Fine." She didn't really care.

They settled on a recent comedy neither of them had seen. It wasn't particularly funny, but at least it whiled away the time. He dragged a hand-knit throw off the back of the couch, told her his mother had knit it and placed it across both their knees. At some point he put an arm around her shoulder and pulled her against him so she was snuggled against his warm, solid bulk.

It felt nice. Warm and safe. She tried not to think about how sexy it was to feel the warmth of his skin beneath her cheek, to smell his unique scent, to hear the steady thud of his heart.

Amazingly, she felt herself begin to relax.

10

ADAM FELT THE change in Serena's breathing and knew the second she fell asleep. Her hair brushed his skin like silk tassels; her soft breath wafted over his chest. He'd never wanted a woman more.

He'd never fought his own urges harder.

She was in his house for protection. She trusted him.

He wished he'd never kissed her. All he could think about when he looked at her was how good she'd tasted. When she was close, like now, he could feel her warmth, the press of her body against his. But this wasn't the time or the place. Damn, he wished he was a pajama-wearing guy simply so he could have lent her something that would cover that spectacular body a little more fully. Instead he'd been tormented by the smooth expanse of her long legs, the shape of her breasts in their natural, braless shape. Even her feet turned him on. They were dainty feet, the nails painted pink.

When she was like this, vulnerable and soft, she no longer reminded him of Madame D, but he recognized that her appeal was much more dangerous. As he glimpsed the real woman behind the efficient, tough-by-day coach, he saw a woman he could seriously fall for. Brainy, sweet, sexy, vulnerable. He almost wished she hadn't shared the awful details of her childhood. Knowing where she'd come from and how brave she'd been only made him feel more committed to keeping her safe. She hadn't known enough of that in her life.

He didn't have time for this. Not for lust or soft feelings. Not when she needed him to be fully alert to any danger.

He'd experienced a bad moment when he'd heard movement in the cottage, thought her supposed safe house had been breached. He wasn't a violent man—had fired his piece maybe three times in his career. But he'd known as he'd taken his firearm in hand that he'd seriously hurt anyone who tried to injure Serena.

She sighed in her sleep and her arm reached around him, resting on his belly as though they were used to being wrapped together. It had been a long time since he'd felt this. Wanted this.

He punched down the volume on the movie. Settled back and held her while she slept.

One useful aspect of his frequent bouts of insomnia was how much time he could spend in the quiet hours of the night working on cases. Serena's case was more difficult in that she was being secretive with facts he needed to know. Like the names of her clients, for a start.

If only she would trust him.

He glanced down at the top of her head, all shining hair, the tip of one ear just visible. He had no idea what was going on in that maddening control-freak head of hers but obviously it was not easy for her to trust.

From the beginning he'd sensed a wariness about her that made him suspect her toughness was a defense she'd learned at an early age. Probably under difficult circumstances.

Now he knew her story, and all the wariness, the

glimpses of steel, made sense. This soft woman beside him had not only survived a bad childhood, she'd managed to put it behind her and thrive. He admired the hell out of her.

MAX PHONED AT seven-thirty in the morning.

"Good news. The office is clean. No surveillance equipment anywhere."

"Okay. Thanks."

"I've installed a pinhole camera that catches the office entrance and part of the assistant's desk. One more that covers the entrance to Serena's office. Figured she'd freak if I put a camera right inside her inner sanctum."

"You're probably right. Get back to me when you've checked out her rez."

"Will do."

He relayed the information to Serena, who sat at his kitchen table eating granola and yogurt. She was back in her skirt and blouse from the day before, the suit jacket neatly hung on the back of the chair.

"That's good news, right?"

"Mixed. Means nobody's been spying on you in your office but also means we've got nothing to go on. So in that way, not good news."

In spite of the couple of hours of sleep she'd caught curled up against him, there was a strained look around her eyes that was part stress and part sleep deprivation. "I think I'd rather it was my office than my home. I really hope I haven't been starring in my own reality show for some pervert who hid cameras in my apartment."

"Yeah." He couldn't even think about her starring in some perv's private movie without wanting to hit something.

"What time do you have to go to work?"

"Later."

She stood up. Cleaned up her stuff and put it in the dishwasher. "I really need to get to the gym. And then the office." She said the words assertively, as though she knew he was going to argue with her. Which he did.

"Let's wait until we hear from Max."

"But my office is fine."

"I know. Let's just figure out what we're dealing with. I've seen you. You can work anywhere."

"I hate this," she muttered. "I want to work out." But she didn't argue with him, simply went to her briefcase and hauled out her laptop. Within minutes, she was settled at his desk, tapping away at her computer, her phone near to hand.

He made another pot of coffee. Put a mug in front of her and she nodded absently.

Max didn't call.

He came by the house before ten. Accepted a cup of coffee. He walked right over to Serena, who had risen from the desk, and pulled her into his arms for a hug. Adam tried to ignore the stab of jealousy in his chest. Serena had said there'd never been anything romantic between her and Max and he believed her. He suspected his visceral reaction to seeing her in the arms of another man stemmed from being unable to pull her into his own arms. Not only for a comforting hug but for so much more.

He might not be the noblest guy on the block but he had standards. He couldn't take advantage of the woman when she was staying under his roof. So he turned away to pour himself another coffee until he was certain the embrace was over.

Max sat on the couch looking immaculate in a professionally pressed white shirt and gray flannels. Serena sat across from him on the chair. Adam remained standing.

He felt a tension in Max that he didn't like. Suspected Serena was picking up on it, too.

Max didn't waste any time beating around the bush. "Your apartment was also clean. No bugs or cameras."

She blew out a breath.

"In order to respect your privacy we've installed a camera that will provide surveillance at the entrance to your apartment. There's no coverage inside."

"But why would you bother?" she asked. "He's obviously some lonely guy with a computer and a fixation who happened to see me yesterday and recognize me. Honestly, I think we're blowing this all out of proportion."

"I did find something," he said. Which meant he'd gone along himself, as Adam had hoped he would. He opened his sleek silver space-age briefcase and removed a transparent plastic evidence bag. Inside the bag was a sheet of paper. He placed the item on the table. "This was taped to your apartment door."

It was a plain sheet of letter-size printer paper. On it in black felt pen was a hand-drawn smiley face.

Serena gasped and put her hand out, only to snatch it back.

"He's letting you know he can get to you," Adam said, keeping his voice calm with an effort. He wanted to rail and curse and find this asshole and beat him to a pulp. Instead he had to sound calm for Serena's sake. Stay calm and focused so he could actually be some use to her. By, say, finding the guy.

"How would he know where I live? And even if he did, my building's secure. There are so many fobs and warning signs posted I'm surprised any of us can get in." Her voice was shaky and she was as white as the paper on which the perp had scrawled.

"I don't know, but we're going to find out," he promised her. He turned to Max.

"Anybody touch that paper?"

"None of my team. We all wear gloves. I bagged it personally. Before we got there?" He shrugged. "Who knows?"

"What time did you go?"

"We arrived at 8:37 a.m. Departed the scene twenty-two minutes later."

Max returned her keys and fob, placing them on the table beside the bag. "I got into the building and I don't live there. Probably somebody did what you did and lent their keys out."

"Or a person going in held the door for somebody," Adam added. "Even though we tell people all the time not to do that for security reasons, a lot of people are too polite to shut the door in a person's face."

Serena was staring at the drawn face with its obscene smile as though she couldn't look away. He reached for it, pulled it out of her sight line. "I'll take that in, check for fingerprints." He wasn't hopeful. He suspected the smiley-face guy, like Max's security team, wore gloves when he worked.

Max sipped coffee absently, then said, "Your stalker has now proven he can get close to you. Physically. He's escalating the threat. First it was email, pretty vague. Anyone with a computer connection or a library card could send you an email. Then he got personal. Sent you a text on your phone. Made it clear he'd somehow seen you yesterday. Knew what you were wearing."

"Yeah," she whispered, looking down at her blue skirt.

"Now he's showing up at your residence." Max glanced between Serena and Adam, a furrow drawing his brows together. "I don't like it."

"That would be two of us," Serena agreed.

"Make it three," he said. Her face was still pale but she had a hold of herself. "Now we've got a camera on your door so if it happens again, we've got him."

She nodded.

"Your building will have security cameras. You know where they are?"

"I think only at the main entrance. Maybe the parking garage." She shrugged helplessly. "I've never paid attention."

"Well, Mr. Smiley got in somehow. I'll get hold of the footage. Maybe if you review it, you'll see someone you recognize. You left your apartment at six-thirty yesterday morning, right?"

She nodded. "And you found it at 8:37 a.m. this morning?"

"Right," said Max. "Twenty-six hours. Pretty big window."

MAX CLOSED HIS fancy case and stood up, looking like an international superspy. "The invitation stands. If you want to stay with me for a while, I've got plenty of room."

"No. I refuse to be frightened out of my own home," she said. "I'm going back to my apartment."

Max and Adam exchanged glances.

"Then I'm coming with you," Adam said, surprising himself.

"What?"

"Until we catch this weasel, I'm moving into your apartment."

"But—"

"Or you can stay here."

"This is ridiculous."

"You're not a stupid woman. For some reason, this guy's

going crazy and fast. I don't know how he's seeing you. How he got access to your apartment. Maybe he lives in the building. Could be one of your neighbors, a caretaker, delivery guy."

Her face was lined by doubt. She turned to her old friend. "What do you think, Max?"

"Adam's right. You shouldn't be alone. He's a good cop. He'll watch your back. But if you prefer one of my guys, just say the word."

"No. If I have to have someone living with me, at least I know Adam." She attempted a smile. "And I won't feel so obliged. I look at it as a trade—personal coaching for bodyguard services."

"That's my girl," Max said. He glanced at his watch. "Let me know if there's anything else I can do."

"I can't be with her all the time," Adam said, voicing his thoughts. "Could you spring for somebody to keep an eye on Serena at work?"

"What?" she gasped. "You mean like a babysitter?"

"I mean like a security guard."

Before she could rant at him, Max interrupted. "We're not talking rent-a-cops here, Serena. We'll send in somebody who you can say is an accountant doing your books or an intern or something. Nobody outside this room will know the truth. That he's a trained security professional." He nodded at both of them. "I'll have someone there by this afternoon."

"Thanks," Adam said, knowing that it would be a huge relief to have someone watching Serena during the hours he had to do his own job. And part of that job was tracking down whoever was messing with his sexy performance coach.

Max turned to Serena. "I mean it. You need anything, call me."

"I will."

With a wave, he was gone.

Serena stared once more at the smiley face grinning up at her in a gruesome parody of itself. Then she turned away with a shudder.

He scooped up the evidence bag and placed it in his beaten-up old leather briefcase.

"I want to take this down to the precinct and get it checked out right away. How about I take you home and then I'll pick you up in a couple of hours and drive you to work."

"I'm perfectly capable—"

"Stop being a pain in the ass."

She huffed out an irritated breath. "Fine."

11

SERENA HAD NEVER felt unsafe in her apartment. She lived on the eighteenth floor of an exclusive building. Her neighbors, mostly executives or retirees, were lovely people.

Now someone had invaded her space.

She didn't like the feeling of vulnerability that gave her.

As they drove toward her home, she and Adam didn't talk much. She was aware of Adam brooding beside her. They parked in the visitor area and he walked around to open the door for her, scanning the vicinity with a practiced eye before allowing her to exit the car.

This must be what it's like to be royalty or a celebrity, she thought as he put an arm across her back and hustled her to the front door. Her key fob was already in her hand, so they scooted right into the wood-and-marble lobby. She saw him glance around and knew he wasn't admiring the decor. He was checking for cameras. As she'd suspected, there was one only outside the front door.

The elevator seemed small with Adam inside it. He took up a lot of space and that somehow made her feel breathless. She caught him looking at her and when she returned the gaze, he glanced away.

He stepped out of the elevator first, scanned right and

left before nodding to her to follow him. She unlocked her heavy front door, imagining how she'd have felt if she'd been the one to find that awful face taped there. Adam watched every move. She suspected he was gauging the security.

Once inside, he said, "May I take a look around?"

She didn't argue, merely nodded. She hoped he would look in all the closets and under the beds so she didn't have to.

It didn't take more than five minutes for Adam to check every room.

"Nice place," he said. "And it checks out."

Then they stood together in the foyer. "I'm so sorry to put you to so much trouble," she said.

Her cell phone sounded, indicating she had a text message. She willed her hand not to shake as she pulled out the smartphone and checked the message. Adam watched her, grim and alert.

"Oh, thank heaven. It's just Lisa checking in. She doesn't know about the creepy text yet. She wouldn't know this would freak me out." She put a hand to her head. "I've got to get a grip."

He grasped her shoulders with two hands. "You're doing great."

Their gazes connected and she saw such strong feeling there that she said, "Adam." Just that one word, uttered in a breathless tone, and suddenly he was crushing her against him, his mouth coming down hard on hers.

She wrapped herself around him, clinging, grasping his jacket, pulling him closer. His mouth was both fierce and tender at once as he plundered and took. Her response was so strong she shocked herself. She was wild with lust, crazy for him.

Part of her suspected that stress and fear were being

channeled into sexual need so strong she was literally aching to be taken. She didn't really care. It was so much better to feel this raging excitement than the gnawing fear.

She moaned against his mouth when he pulled slowly away. He stared down at her, breathing heavily, obviously as shocked by their over-the-top passion as she was.

"I would apologize for that except that I don't think I can."

She put a hand up to his face, all craggy and warm. "Funny. I was thinking of thanking you."

He chuckled at that. "You are one hell of a woman, you know that?"

Then he did the strangest thing. He lifted her hand from his cheek and kissed the open palm. "I'll see you later."

Max called her soon after Adam left. "I've got someone for you," he said. "Name's Mark Hardy. Former marine. Also has a degree in accounting, which comes in handy."

"I already have an accountant," she said, feeling more and more like other people were taking over her life.

"Maybe you can give him a bogus project to work on. Doesn't matter. He'll arrive before you in the morning and check the place out. He'll leave with you at the end of the day and see you off the premises. He'll make sure you get home okay."

"What if I don't want to go home?" She knew she was being unreasonable but she felt as though she were under house arrest.

Max was eminently reasonable and acted as though her pissiness were perfectly normal. "Wherever you go in the day you should take him with you. Maybe calling him an intern is a better idea. Or you've hired a junior performance coach. You're trying him out on probation. Or maybe he's writing a book about you and wants to follow you everywhere. He'll follow your lead. Have a private meeting with him this afternoon and figure it out."

"This is going to cause trouble with my assistant, you know. She wants to train as a performance coach."

"You were always good at HR problems in business school. You'll figure it out."

"I want my real life back."

"You'll get it. Be patient."

She'd never been very good with patience.

After a long shower, she did her hair and makeup and changed into a pair of houndstooth slacks and a crisp white shirt. Put on some discreet gold jewelry and Chanel flats. Somehow, feeling put together physically helped her feel put together mentally. If she was also wearing some of the nicest underwear she owned, the stuff she'd paid an absurd amount for in Paris, that was her business.

She double-checked that her guest bedroom was dust-free and made the bed with fresh sheets. She put out fresh towels in the second bathroom. That steamy kiss had been amazing, but she wasn't sure this was the time to start an affair with a cop who had assigned himself the role of her personal bodyguard.

But then, she wasn't sure she had the strength to resist if he tried to seduce her.

The cleaners had been only a couple of days earlier, so the place was spotless.

Oh, no, she thought. The cleaners. They had a key to her home. She'd have to tell Adam. Maria and Esperanza were two lovely women from Colombia who'd been her housekeepers for a couple of years now. No doubt Adam would brand them as members of a drug cartel or something and end up scaring them away.

She made herself a sandwich and, while she ate her lunch, tried to figure out how to present Mark to her assistant without divulging his real identity and purpose in her office.

She finished the sandwich, ate an apple, brewed tea and was still no closer to a solution. Finally, she decided there wasn't one. She was going to tell Lisa the truth.

It flicked across her mind that Lisa had dropped important files off at her apartment a couple of times. She could easily talk her way into the building.

In order to leave a scrawled happy face on her boss's door? No. Serena made a decision right there that she was going to continue to trust the people she was closest to until there was a reason not to.

She felt better once she'd made that decision. A little more in control. She wasn't prepared to let a nameless coward damage relationships that were important to her.

Adam arrived soon after one. The second she saw him her stomach went jumpy. He gave her a slow, sexy grin. "Hi."

"Hi."

He held up an overnight bag. "I packed a few things."

"Okay." He took the bag straight to the guest room. She was relieved he didn't assume he'd be sharing her bed tonight based on that deep hot kiss. Sex with Adam—as hot as it would no doubt be—would only complicate her already messed-up life.

As he drove her to her office, he said, "I talked to your building superintendent. Said there'd been an incident without giving any specifics. You've got security cameras outside the front door and the parking garage and there's one in the foyer I didn't spot. No cameras on the individual floors, unfortunately. Anyway, we can review the tapes. See if you recognize anyone."

She nodded. Dreaded the idea of recognizing someone, perhaps someone she knew and liked, sneaking in to leave her such an eerie message. She much preferred the theory that her threatening texter was a stranger to her, someone who'd seen her at a public event and got a kinky thrill sending her uncomfortable messages.

She also hoped they found the person very soon. Before she lost any more of her autonomy.

When they got to her office, Adam insisted on coming in with her. Lisa glanced up in surprise when he entered. "Hi, Lisa," she said. "You remember Adam?"

"Yes. Of course. Hello." Lisa must have been wondering what was going on. Serena had been with Adam at the end of her workday yesterday, called this morning to say she'd be a few hours late in and then turned up with him in tow. Lisa was too much of a professional to reveal even the tiniest hint of her thoughts, which Serena appreciated.

"Hi."

She led Adam into her office to keep up the pretense that he was here on business. "I could give you some reading material to help you focus on peak performance," she said.

When she turned, he'd shut the door. "I don't think I need reading material," he said as he pulled her into his arms and proceeded to demonstrate peak kissing performance.

When he pulled slowly away, leaving her stunned and half reeling, she said, "This is very inconvenient timing."

"I know. It sucks." He kissed her again, swiftly. "See you tonight."

SHE FIXED HER LIPSTICK, checked the mirror she kept in her desk to make sure her hair wasn't mussed, then walked to the door. "Lisa, can I talk to you in my office for a second?"

"Sure."

Lisa came in, a notebook and pen in hand.

"Sit down."

"You're not firing me, are you?" Lisa asked, her face growing suddenly pale, her eyes widening.

"Firing you? God, no."

"Oh, good. I really wish I hadn't brought up the idea of training to be a coach yesterday. It was bad timing. I am really sorry if I offended you in any way."

"No. No. It's my fault. What's going on with me has nothing to do with you. And I'm flattered that you want to move up in the business. Truly."

Lisa nodded, looking far from relieved.

Serena made a decision right then and there. "And I've decided to take you up on your suggestion. You're right. I'm swamped and turning business away. You can work with me, train with me, and soon you'll build your own client list."

Lisa's expression changed from carefully neutral to overjoyed. "Really?" Her smile was so wide it looked painful. "Wow. Thanks. I'm so excited. I've got a ton of ideas and I'll work really hard to prove myself to you."

"You already have or I wouldn't be offering you this opportunity."

"Right. Awesome. Thanks."

She knew that if she trusted Lisa enough to bring her into the business, she needed to trust her enough to tell her the truth. "But there's something going on that might make you change your mind about working with me."

"I can't imagine."

"You know those emails? The creepy ones I've been getting?"

Lisa frowned. "Yeah. Of course."

"Well, yesterday I got a text message. Obviously from the same person." It was hard for her even to talk about this. She swallowed. "The text mentioned what I was wearing yesterday. It kind of freaked me out."

"Oh, my God." Lisa's hand went to her heart and a look of horror replaced the happy smile of a moment ago.

"You know how the emails always end with a happy face?"

Lisa nodded.

"Well, so did the text. And then this morning there was a hand-drawn happy face taped to my apartment door."

Lisa's face drained of color. "Serena, you need to go to the police."

"Adam is the police."

"Oh, right."

"And my good friend Max Varo owns a top security firm. He's arranged for an ex-marine security expert named Mark to come hang out in the office and keep an eye on us. He'll be arriving this afternoon."

"He's what, like a bodyguard?"

"Yes."

"Wow."

"As I said, if all of this makes you too uncomfortable, I perfectly understand if you want to take some time off. Now that the crazy emailer has proven he has access to me, I have to wonder if you could be in any danger."

Lisa rose. "I am not a person who runs away when people I care about are in trouble. Tell me what I can do."

It was such a simple statement but Serena felt ridiculously cheered by the support.

"Thanks. The best thing you can do is act like nothing out of the ordinary has happened. And keep your eyes and ears open."

"Oh, don't worry." She fiddled with her notebook and then said, "Do you have any idea who could be doing this?"

"I wish I did." Oh, it was nice to have someone to talk to who wasn't going to boss her around. And who was a woman. "What about you? You're observant and you've studied psychology. Has anyone seemed off at all to you?"

"I can't think of anyone, no."

"I hate to even ask, but Marcus has the skills to send untraceable emails and so on. And those video games he invents are awful, violent things."

Lisa's eyes opened in obvious shock. "Marcus Lemming?" She was already shaking her head. "Marcus is the sweetest, gentlest person I've ever known. And he thinks the world of you. He'd never do anything to hurt you."

She was pleased, of course, that Lisa didn't think Marcus could be behind the harassment, but another unpleasant idea raised its head. The suspicion that her soon-to-be partner had a crush on one of their biggest clients.

MARK TURNED OUT to be a sweet-faced man in his mid-thirties. She'd been worried that he'd have a marines haircut and military bearing that would give him away immediately, but of course Max owned the best security company in town. They didn't go in for obvious. Mark wore a suit that couldn't hide his muscular build, but nothing else about him suggested he was anything other than the office clerk he was pretending to be. His hair was average. His looks were average. His voice was, well, average. She had no clue from his speech what part of the country he was from. He acted polite and low-key. She thought she'd have trouble spotting him in a crowd.

He was, in a word, perfect.

He took his assigned desk and moved it slightly so he had better sight lines. Then he settled behind the second desk she kept in the front area, where her accountant or the odd contract admin she hired to help with big projects worked when they were in the office.

She gave Mark a spreadsheet on her book sales to update. He seemed perfectly happy with the menial task of inputting data, though she noticed he took frequent breaks to walk around, check what was happening in the hallway, glance out the window. At first he unnerved her. Then after a while she got used to it.

For a woman who prided herself on independence, she now had a daytime bodyguard and a nighttime bodyguard.

At least one of them was a relaxing, nonthreatening presence.

_12_

NOTHING HAPPENED ALL that day. As the hours progressed, Serena began to feel more and more as if she and Adam and Max had overreacted.

Serena worked quietly in the office. The only thing on her calendar for the day was a networking event in the afternoon.

At four she came out of her office and Mark immediately rose and stepped out from behind his desk. "I've got a networking event to go to," she told both Mark and Lisa.

Her assistant frowned. "Are you sure you should go?"

"Yes. I refuse to cancel a single engagement. If I do, my stalker will think he's winning whatever bizarre game he's playing."

Lisa didn't look entirely convinced. "Don't forget you're not dealing with a normal person here. Your behavior could be taken as a challenge."

"I suppose." Lisa did have a degree in psychology, she reminded herself. "But I still think my best defense is to ignore him. Carry on. Let him see his tactics aren't working."

"Where is this event?" Mark asked.

It was in a small ballroom at one of the big hotels. To

her consternation he radioed their plans to somebody or other. She felt as if she was being watched from all sides. Even the good guys were spying on her!

"If anyone asks, you're a journalist writing a profile of me for a business magazine," she told him on the way over. He drove carefully and she got the feeling he was checking constantly to see if they were being followed.

"Which magazine?" he asked.

"I don't know."

"May I suggest a trade publication? I'll say I'm a freelance writer working on contract."

"Good. Perfect." They agreed on a large industrial magazine and that they wouldn't mention the name of the publication unless pressed to do so.

The ruse was perfectly acceptable. And she found herself relaxing as she made the rounds of the room, talking to people she liked, did business with or might do business with in the future. Mark was always nearby, but not following her around like a dog on a leash.

"Who's that nice piece of eye candy?" Janine Estevez asked Serena when they crossed paths. Janine was also a business coach, though not nearly as successful. It was obvious that she was envious of Serena's career. Enough to sabotage her? Enough to send cruel messages?

"He's writing a profile about me for a business magazine," she said, sticking to the story they'd made up earlier.

"Lucky you." The words weren't sneered, exactly, but Serena could detect a certain bitterness.

"And how are things going with you?"

"Great," Janine gushed. "I'm going to Hawaii in a few weeks with my new boyfriend. He's a salesman I coached. He was struggling then. Now he's the top guy in his firm."

"That's wonderful," Serena said. "Isn't it fantastic when we truly make a difference in people's lives?"

Janine agreed that it was and they moved on. And Serena reminded herself that she had to stop suspecting every person she came into contact with of being a crazy stalker.

MARK HANDED HER over to Adam at the end of the day. Honestly, she was starting to feel like a piece of registered mail.

As they were driving back to her place, he reached for her hand. "You all right?"

"Yes." Liar.

"I've arranged for us to view the footage from the surveillance camera in your building."

"All right." She could think of a million unpleasant things she'd rather do than play Spot the Stalker. Maybe he sensed that, because he held her hand the whole way home.

The building superintendent was waiting for them in his office. He was a retired municipal employee and she felt his distress. He liked order and a smoothly run building—and he had the memos to prove it.

"Ms. Long," he said, "I'm sorry to hear you've had a security issue. I'm putting out a memo reminding everyone never to let strangers into the building." He sighed. "But you know what people are like."

She nodded. She'd have protested except that she received that same memo at least once a year. Then there were the memos reminding people to always confirm that the parking gate had closed completely behind them before driving forward. Then there were the memos reminding residents not to leave patio doors open during the summer if they weren't home. And the memos requesting that no one lend out their keys or fobs. She had thought her building was so secure.

"I've got the footage ready to roll on this computer here," he said, ushering her to a desk in a corner.

The recording played like a video. She could push Stop and Play, slow it down or speed it up. They'd requested many hours of footage and she had to look at images from three cameras. They started with the front-door camera. She watched what looked like a grainy black-and-white movie of people coming and going. Her neighbors, friends dropping by, a guy with a cell phone and briefcase whom she recognized as a local realtor, food-delivery people. At Adam's urging she took careful note of all the delivery personnel but there was no one she recognized. She felt as though she were watching the world's most boring home movie. The film skipped slightly around 4:00 p.m. Adam reversed and watched the footage again. Frowning.

He didn't say anything. She continued watching. Yep, the woman who took the Pekingese for a stroll returned after a while. The people who'd left for work returned from work. She watched her neighbors head for their workouts and come back red-faced and glowing. She watched people struggling into her building lugging a week's groceries. She watched and watched. No one appeared on-screen who shouldn't have been there.

Same deal for the other two tapes.

"Okay," Adam said, after her eyes felt as if they'd fall out of her head if she watched one more second of security footage. "Thanks for looking."

He turned to the building manager. "You'll keep this. Right?"

"Yes, of course. Let me know and I'll make it available anytime."

"Thanks."

And they left.

She felt tired, irritable, as though everyone involved in this foolishness—including her—was overreacting.

Her front door was thankfully free of any decoration.

She let out a breath and unlocked her suite. Adam walked right in without an invitation and quickly searched the apartment.

"Everything look okay to you?" he asked.

"Yes."

"Good." He fiddled with his car keys.

"Why did you go back and look at the skipped tape?"

"My guess is that our computer-savvy cyber stalker managed to disable the cameras."

"You can do that?"

"Yes. He'd need a device to deliver an electromagnetic pulse. Max's people could figure out how it was done, but it won't help us find out who."

"So that little movie date was a total waste of time," she said.

"No. If I'm right, we know when your friend visited. Around 4:00 p.m."

"So what?"

"So it's one more piece of the puzzle. Slowly, we will make a picture and then we will get our guy and make him stop."

"I really hope that happens soon."

"Look. I've got hockey practice tonight. Do you want to come with?"

"No. It's about the last thing I want to do. No offense."

He grinned at her. "None taken. Will you be all right if I go?"

"Yes. You should go." She was delighted to find that his idea of security still left her some privacy. "You love your hockey and it would be a sad thing if your performance coach was the reason you couldn't go to practice."

"Promise me you won't go out and you don't let anyone in. Nobody. I don't care how well you know them."

"Except you?" she had to ask.

"Except me, smart-ass. I'll skip the beers with the boys afterward and come straight here. Should get back around ten."

"Yes. That's fine. I'll be up then, or do you want the key?"

"No. I'll buzz up."

"Okay. Have fun."

"Thanks. You try and get some rest. Relax."

He looked as though he might say more. His gaze drifted to her lips and he pulled her to him for a long hard kiss.

SERENA COULDN'T SETTLE. She'd been dying for some time alone after an entire day of people checking up on her. Escorting her—guarding her. Now that she was alone, she suddenly felt vulnerable.

"No." She actually said the word aloud.

No. Fear was not going to get her. Adam was going to sleep at her place. She lived in a mostly secure building and was inside her suite with the door locked. She'd be fine until ten o'clock. Absolutely fine.

What did she always tell her clients? What did she preach in her books, on her blog, in her lectures? Fear itself was the enemy. If she let herself give in and panic, she'd be lost. So she changed out of her dress clothes, put on some comfy sweats.

She decided to start work on next week's blog. She'd write about turning challenges into successes. Hopefully she'd believe her own prose.

As she turned on her computer, she was conscious of a feeling of dread lodging in her belly. Whatever she wrote, she knew *he'd* read it.

But if she didn't post anything on her scheduled day, he'd know that too. And exult in his success.

Okay. She sat down. Resolutely put any thought of fear out of her mind. What would she write about?

She cast about for a topic, thought about her networking afternoon. She liked the topic as it was positive but neutral enough that a creepy stalker wouldn't think it was about him.

Damn, there she was thinking about him again.

She pulled in a breath. Did some positive-thinking calisthenics. Repeated the mantra "I am safe and happy. I am in charge of my own life."

Not exactly the most original self-talk in the world but it helped. She typed.

"The Importance of a Good Network." Wow, that was a lame title. However, she knew it was the best she could do right now, and she'd learned long ago that perfect is the enemy of good. She wrote a shorter-than-usual post, but she wrote it. When she thought about the power of networking, it occurred to her that she'd recently discovered a network she hadn't realized she had. There were people in her life who truly cared about her. Max, Lisa, now Adam. She knew there were plenty more people out there—friends, colleagues, clients—who would happily lend a hand if she asked. As she'd help them. She didn't often think about life that way, but surprisingly, it was true. She had a business network, obviously. But she also had a personal network.

She forgot about Smiley Face reading her words. She imagined a net and all the ways we connect to people, each one a string that ties on to another string, and they weave together and then one day you realize the strength of that net when you fall and it catches you.

Maybe the post was a bit out there, but she'd managed to highlight the importance of connections in business and in one's personal life. Good enough, she decided. She proofed her work and published the post.

It was barely 9:00 p.m. but her eyes were dragging with fatigue. She decided to crawl into bed early with a book. It was an indulgence that she always enjoyed. As soon as Adam arrived, she'd put out the light and sleep.

She washed, brushed her teeth, slipped into her night gear and sorted through the books waiting to be read. She wanted something light, positive, upbeat. A colleague had asked her to write a review for his upcoming book on happiness. That, she decided, was a perfect fit. She would do something useful while reading about happiness.

She snapped on her bedside reading light. Flipped back her bed cover.

And screamed.

13

ADAM SKATED HARD. His lungs were burning; his legs were burning. Before he slammed the puck, he pictured a freakin' happy face painted on it and the adrenaline rush sent the puck flying past the startled goalie and into the net so hard it got pushed out of position.

"Good. Do it again," the coach yelled.

They set up the breakout drill again, transitioning from defense to offense. Dylan and Max set him up and once more he nailed the puck.

"Hey, Shawnigan," Dylan yelled, "you keep that up and the cup's ours this year."

He nodded. Wiped sweat off his face. Skated a few times around the rink for the hell of it and finally clomped off the ice as they changed lines. He chugged water. His cell phone shrilled.

Call display told him it was Serena. Gut instinct told him there was trouble.

"Where are you?" he barked into the phone, anxious to get to her.

"I'm at home." Her voice sounded as if she was barely holding on to control. He could hear a tremor. "Adam, he got into my apartment."

He jumped to his feet, forgot his skates were still on his feet and almost toppled. "He there now?"

"No. He— he left me another message. It was—it was in my bed."

"Don't move. I'll be right there."

"I—I don't think I can move," she said.

"Hang on. Just hang on."

He dragged off his skates, shoved them in his bag, jammed his feet into sneakers and ran. How could he have been so stupid? He never should have left her alone, not when some maniac was out to get her. Never.

"What's up?" Vaguely he was aware of Dylan running behind him.

He didn't turn. "Serena. I'll call when I can."

He broke every speed limit, tore through red lights, screamed to a halt in front of her building and jumped out. Ran to her front door. Buzzed her code.

"Yes?" Her voice sounded tentative.

"Serena, it's me. Adam."

"Come up."

Never had an elevator taken so long to rise. He reached her floor, sprinted down the hall. Banged on her door. Ducked a little to make sure his face was level with her peephole.

The door opened. She stood there, pale but holding it together.

He pulled her to his chest and hugged her long and hard.

"What happened?" he asked at last, reluctantly letting go of her.

"I didn't touch it." She led the way to her bedroom and he followed.

He could see where she'd flipped back the coverlet of her bed. On the pillow was another hand-drawn smiley face. This one had a detail added that hadn't been on the face on the door earlier.

In this drawing the smiley-face mouth dripped red droplets of blood made by a red crayon.

Seeing her reaction to the thing, he once more pulled her to his chest and held tight.

"You still have all your padding on," she protested, but she clung to him anyway.

"All I had time to take off was my skates."

"I can't believe he was here. Inside my home. I feel so violated."

"How did he get in?"

"I don't know. I checked all the windows and the balcony door but they're locked from the inside."

First he bagged the evidence. The horrible smiley face with the fake blood dripping from its mouth. He hid the thing away in his briefcase.

Then he double-checked that she was right. There was no sign of forced entry. He checked the front-door locks. Again, everything looked normal.

"Who else has keys? Apart from you?"

"The cleaners. But they've worked for me for two years. I trust them."

"I'll need their names and contact information. Anybody else?"

"The building superintendent has access, obviously."

"Former lovers? People who've stayed here? Anybody forget to return the key?"

She shook her head.

"You lose your keys recently?"

She glanced at him with impatience. "I'd have told you."

"You have a spare set?"

She nodded. Walked to the kitchen. A rack of keys

hung on one wall. She paused. He watched her spine go stiff. Shit.

She turned, her eyes wide. "They're gone." She turned back. "I can't believe I didn't notice. I always keep the spare on this hook right here." She pointed to an empty spot. "They're the keys I was going to give you! Here are my spare car keys, spare office keys, key to my bike locker and storage locker." Her voice was tight, high. "But no spare to the front door."

"When's the last time you remember using them or lending them out?"

She put a hand to her temple and rubbed as though a headache was forming. "I don't know." He gave her a moment, resisting the urge to comfort her. She needed to think.

"Wait. It was in the summer. I was out of town and asked Lisa to bring up my mail and water the plants on my balcony."

"She give the keys back?"

"Yes. Of course." She glared at him. "And I trust Lisa completely. She's got nothing to do with this fear campaign."

He let that go, knowing there was no point in arguing about whether Lisa could be trusted or not. "Then my best guess is that somebody swiped your keys out of your purse, let themselves into your apartment, got hold of your spare."

"My purse hasn't gone missing. I'd have noticed."

"What about at the gym? Do you lock your purse up?"

"Sure. I have a locker. You bring your own combination lock. But sometimes I forget the lock." She frowned. "I've been known to leave my purse in an unlocked locker. I figure it's a nice club and I feel like I know most of the people who go there in the mornings. So maybe a few times I've been sloppy."

"And at work? Where do you keep your purse when you're at work?"

"In my desk drawer."

"Do you always take it with you wherever you go?"

"No."

"So it's not impossible that someone could have taken your keys, got into your place and returned them without you noticing."

Her forehead creased. "But why leave that stupid picture on my pillow? He must know I'll get the locks changed. He could have waited until I was home." She gulped. "Walked in on me."

"For some reason he doesn't want that. Max was right. He's playing with you. What did those messages say? He wants to teach you about fear. If you didn't know he was tracking you, you wouldn't be afraid. So he's toying with you, playing cat and mouse."

She licked dry lips. Her eyes were wide and dark. "How far is he going to go?"

"I don't know what his plans are," he said evenly. "But he's not getting any further. This stops now."

He pulled out his cell.

"Who are you calling?"

"This isn't simple harassment anymore. He broke into your home and left you a threat. Not calling in the cops officially is no longer an option."

"I hate this."

"I know. But it will be a lot better once we file an official report. I'll be able to work on your case in regular hours. Not call in favors."

Then he called a twenty-four-hour locksmith.

When the locksmith left three hours later, she had a brand-new deadbolt, new keys and a super-fancy invincible security lock on the inside of her door.

And such fury in her gut she could barely stand it, because the texting, emailing, smiley-facing stalker had won this round.

He'd taught her fear.

14

"I AM SO glad you're here," she said to Adam, hating that she needed him in order to feel safe.

"I'm not going anywhere," he said, and then he pulled her to him.

"I'm so scared," she admitted against his chest.

"I know."

"I don't want to be scared," she said through gritted teeth.

"I know that, too."

She raised her face toward him in mute invitation. He didn't avail himself of the offer, though she saw want and need burning in his eyes. She closed her own and put her lips on his. He resisted for only a moment and then, suddenly, his passion was unleashed. He kissed her as though he'd die if he didn't. He pulled her against him with no finesse or elegance. He still wore padding from the practice, black shorts and a faded hockey jersey from his college days. She smelled the sweat of his workout and the banked fury that heated his skin.

"I don't want to take advantage," he said, pulling away from her with an effort.

"Tough. I want to be taken advantage of," she said,

amazed at the huskiness in her tone. "And you're exactly the man to do it."

"Oh, I am."

His hands, those gorgeous big hands, began to roam, first grasping her hips, then tracing the sides of her waist, cupping her breasts. Every part of her felt hot and needy. "I need a shower," he gasped.

"Later." And she began to tug the jersey up and over his head.

There was no finesse to her movements. She was wild with need. She didn't care that she'd lost control. Didn't care that he could see it. Tiny grunts and groans came from her throat as she tugged at his clothing, frustrated every time she released a garment only to find more padding or another layer.

"Am I ever going to get you naked?" she demanded.

"Oh, yes," he promised, and began pulling at his own clothing, seeming as lust addled as she was.

At last she had him naked and she could understand why she'd been so wild to get him there. The man was ridiculously, over-the-top gorgeous.

There are men who look better in clothes.

Adam was not one of those men.

Clothed, he was a big good-looking tough-guy type.

Naked, he was an ancient god. Huge, muscled, broad of shoulder and lean of hip. Once more the image of Thor flitted through her mind. Yes, she thought, that would suit him. He was more Norse than Greek. Rough, rugged, a man who took what he wanted and damn the consequences.

She very much hoped that what he wanted was her.

She loved every inch of him. And there were a lot of inches. The length of his torso, the strong arms, those muscled legs that could skate the length of a rink in seconds and could race to her side the minute she called. She loved his big capable hands and the feet that kept him rooted. And she loved the gorgeous cock now standing proud. When she circled him with her hand, his skin was hot, and he was as stiff as iron. At her touch he groaned.

"We shouldn't be doing this," he managed, his eyes barely focused.

Oh, she loved her power.

Maybe he was right but lust felt so much better than fear that she said, "Yes. We should."

"Okay," he groaned. "You've convinced me." And just like that his mood changed from one of resistance to all-in. He removed her hand, kissed the palm. "If you hold me much longer, this will be over too fast," he said.

She definitely didn't want that, so she kept her hands to herself. Sort of. She couldn't help the way they roamed over his chest and shoulders and back and belly. She was careful, however, not to go too near the hot zone.

He began to strip off her clothes. It didn't take nearly as long, since she was already dressed for bed. A lift, a pull, silk trailing over her skin like a warm breeze and then she was as naked as he was.

When he looked at her, she felt momentarily shy.

Until she saw the way he was looking at her. With hunger, lust and something softer that she couldn't name. He reached out and touched her breast. "You are even more beautiful than I imagined," he said.

Then he closed the distance between their bodies and she felt enveloped by his warmth and strength. She was a tall woman and she liked to think she was fairly strong, but in Adam's arms she felt tiny. Cherished.

She considered herself as much of a feminist as the next CEO, but here in the comfort of her bedroom she quite liked feeling small and cherished.

She reached behind them and flipped the duvet, consciously ignoring what had greeted her there the last time she'd done so. If anyone could make her forget the gruesome discovery, it was Adam.

Adam, whose eyes blazed into hers as he lowered her to the bed.

His eyes were like the sky at midnight. Deep, almost black, but with devil lights dancing in their depths. She reached up to touch the craggy planes of his face, and then she lost sight of his eyes as he leaned forward and kissed her.

His big body settled beside her on the bed. He touched her breasts again. It was as though he could never have his fill of them. He began kissing his way down her body, leaving a shivery trail as he excited every inch of skin he touched.

When he reached her thighs, he parted them gently and she felt herself opening for him, knowing she'd give him everything she had.

He took his time, kissing her thighs, lapping at the soft, exquisitely sensitive skin. As he traveled slowly north, she was so fired up she thought she might explode before he even reached his target.

When he rose over her most private parts, she felt him gazing down at her where she was spread before him. He touched her gently, spreading her folds, and she moaned helplessly. Then he lowered his head.

"Oh, yes," she said, sighing as his tongue touched her where she was so hot and so needy.

He lapped at her, licking and inciting while the dark excitement built within her. Her hips began to thrust in time with his tongue, and then, to her shock, she felt him thrust two fingers up inside her, rubbing her G-spot. Even if she'd had the inclination to resist—to drag things out—

she couldn't have held out against the twin assaults of his tongue and those wonderful rubbing fingers.

Her breath came in harsh gasps. She couldn't stop her hips from dancing an intimate tango with his mouth. When he increased the rhythm of both tongue and deep stroking fingers, nothing could stop the body-clenching, sweat-drenching, bone-deep howl of her climax. She felt as though every part of her had dissolved. She was a wet, boneless puddle.

She'd never felt so good.

Except that there was an emptiness within her. And one very horny man was kissing his way back up her body. She felt him quivering with need and the hardness that nudged her hip was of the iron variety.

When his face was level with hers, he growled in her ear, "Do you have anything?"

"Do I have anything?" she repeated, pretending to think deeply. "Well, I have a good personality. A healthy business. A pretty good net worth. I have friends I—"

"I am never letting you come first again," he groaned.

She laughed, feeling ridiculously happy for a woman whose life was quite possibly in danger. She reached over his hot muscular torso to her bedside table and opened the drawer. Handed him a condom.

The ripping of the package sent a quiver through her already quivery insides. Then he was on top of her, nudging open her thighs once more.

When he entered her, she felt for a second that she wouldn't be able to take all of him. He was so big, so hard, but despite his obvious need, he didn't rush her. He took his time easing himself into her and all the while, he kissed her mouth, caressed her breasts, told her in the earthiest ways that her body pleased him.

When he was settled deep inside and she felt full and

complete, he began to move. Instinctively, she moved with him, meeting his thrusts with increasing urgency as her own passion built yet again.

As deep inside her body as he was, she needed him deeper still. She hooked her heels around the back of his hips and held on, urging him ever deeper. A drip of sweat fell onto her as she felt him respond, thrusting up and hard into her again and again.

The tidal wave began to build again. She felt her inner muscles begin to tighten around him, felt her need spiral as she began to lose control.

A wild woman took her over. She began to buck against him. His shoulder brushed against her mouth and she sank her teeth into it.

In response he tightened his grip on her and let himself off his leash. He thrust into her for all he was worth, with no finesse or care. It was exactly, she thought, how the thunder god would mate. Raw, dark and powerful.

She was being pulled out of herself into some mystical place. She felt his force, couldn't resist it, and then her head fell back and dark passion took her over until she cried out once more. In the echo of her own cries she heard his deep guttural moan as they tumbled off the edge of the world.

"THAT WAS AMAZING." His voice rumbled in her ear like the low roll of thunder.

"Mmm," she said. Normally she had a wide vocabulary but right now *mmm* was all she had left in stock.

There was a silence punctuated by pounding hearts gradually slowing and heavy breathing easing to something approaching normal. Her neatly made bed was a mess of tangled sheets. Her tidy floor was a minefield of hockey padding and clothing.

Her comfortable, orderly life was in shambles.

She breathed deeply of chaos.

"Mmm," she said again, then managed to add, "I think I went somewhere I've never been before. Somewhere not on Earth."

"You weren't worried I'd choke under pressure?" he challenged her.

"What?"

"You've been telling me how I have this fear of failure."

She raised herself up on one elbow. Looked him right in the eye.

"You don't have fear of failure," she told Adam. "What you have is a classic case of fear of success."

"That's the stupidest thing I've ever heard. Who's afraid of succeeding?"

"Oh, you'd be surprised. Sometimes there's comfort in the familiar even if it means settling for mediocrity. When a person succeeds, it changes the dynamics of their relationships, makes them vulnerable in ways—"

"OH, MY GOD," he said, falling back onto the pillow. Comfort in mediocrity. Hadn't he witnessed that his whole life? His mother telling his father that it was the foot soldiers who won the war? He heard his mother's voice suddenly in his head, almost like a whisper. *Not everyone can be captain, honey.* But she'd been talking to his dad, not to him. To his father, who'd spent an entire career in law enforcement and watched younger, smarter, better-educated guys move up ahead of him on the force.

"You look like you might be having a breakthrough," she said.

"It's quite the night for breakthroughs," he countered, getting a kick on the shin for his trouble.

"You know that 'aha' moment you mentioned?"

She nodded.

"The chills down the back of the neck?" She looked so beautiful lying there, so feminine and soft and yet so capable and strong. Her eyes were alight as he told her about his epiphany. "It's about my dad. Well, and my mom, I guess. All my life I wanted to be exactly like my dad." He shook his head. How had he never seen this before?

"And my dad is a great guy. He was also a good cop. Solid, reliable. The kind of man who makes a perfect beat cop. He follows the book. He'd never lie or cheat or steal. He's the original honest cop."

She nodded, listening. Her hand settled on his chest and he reached up to clasp it.

"Other guys would get promoted over his head. He'd come home and tell my mother about it and she'd always say something like 'It's the soldiers in the front line who win a war.'" He shook his head, playing with her breast absently. "I heard that message over and over again. Somehow it was nobler to be a foot soldier. That becoming a general was getting above yourself."

She reached over with her free hand and rubbed his shoulder. "And can you see how that might play into your issues on the ice?"

"Yep. It's okay to be part of a winning team, but I'd better not get too big for my boots. Mom might cut me down to size."

"Is that what she used to do? Or still does?"

"No. It's not that she's cutting me down—it's that she's so busy building my dad up that somehow I got the idea that I shouldn't ever try to be better than he was." He felt as though it was getting hard to breathe. "And I'm not. He was and is a good and decent man. I'd trust him with my life."

"Okay, then." She tapped his chest softly. "Why are

your muscles tensing up as you talk about this? Why is your voice sounding strained?"

He covered her hand with his own. Held on. "When I got promoted to detective, you know what I did?"

She shook her head. "No."

"I went home and threw up. I was sure they'd picked the wrong man, that I couldn't do it." He released her hand and began playing with her fingers. "The truth was, I didn't want to get above myself. Or, more importantly, get above my father."

"This is quite the epiphany you're having," she commented.

He turned to look at her, with her hair all over the place and her lips swollen from kissing him. Still, her eyes were those of his sexy performance coach. "You don't look surprised at all. You already knew this, didn't you?"

"I'm not the one who needs to figure these things out. You are." She reached over and nipped his chin between her fingers. "I like to think that I can guide a client a little, but I try not to dominate the process."

He tried to stifle a grin but didn't manage it.

Of course, she caught him. "What?"

"It's nothing. The verb you used. *Dominate*."

"What about it?"

"I— The first time we met, you reminded me of a dominatrix I once arrested. Madame D. She had the same cool sexiness. The same streak of steel."

"I remind you of a dominatrix?" She didn't seem thrilled by the comparison.

"She wasn't what you'd imagine. There was nothing cheap looking or outwardly tough about her. It was only when you got to know her you saw the way she liked to control a man."

"Did she control you?" she asked coolly, as though it didn't matter at all to her, but somehow he knew it did.

"No! I arrested her. She had some clients who were very big-time. Powerful, influential men. Even though she made a fortune tying them up and whipping them, she got greedy and started secretly photographing and then blackmailing them. One of them finally got tired of paying."

"So he went to the police? That was gutsy."

"No. He hired a hit man to get rid of her."

"Oh."

"Yeah. Luckily for Madame D, the hit man was already on our radar for other reasons. When we arrested him, he told us about the hit and worked with us. We got the guy who organized the hit, not to mention Madame D and her extensive library of photographs and video recordings."

"Whatever happened to her?"

"Since she wasn't having sex with these men, what she was doing wasn't prostitution. It's tough to prosecute. The blackmail was the obvious crime, and there was a lot of pantie wetting among some pretty high-profile men. Men you've heard of, who have families and attend church regularly. Amazingly, Madame D disappeared one day."

"Murdered?"

"No. I hear she turned up in Eastern Europe. Somebody with deep pockets and a desire to keep his secrets under wraps probably arranged and paid for her disappearance." He shook his head. "She sure was a sexy woman, though."

"So you had a crush on a dominatrix," she said. "Interesting." She was quiet for a moment. "But not as interesting as discovering the source of those destructive messages you've been sending yourself."

"Wow." He thought about it. "So now that I know this, will I be cured?"

"I don't know. Will you?"

"I feel like I need, I don't know, permission or something."

"Maybe you need to have a conversation," she suggested.

"With him?"

They exchanged a look. He closed his eyes. Of course. "With my mom."

15

"MOM? YOU HOME?"

His mother came out of the kitchen, wiping flour from her hands with a tea towel patterned with birds of North America. Her face lit up when she saw him. "Darling. How wonderful to see you again so soon. I'm only sorry your father's not here. He's off doing the planting at a seniors' residence."

"I'm glad I caught you alone. I want to talk to you." After his breakthrough last night he'd been longing to have this conversation. Something of his urgency must have come through.

Her bright smile dimmed. "Is everything all right?"

"Yes. Everything's fine. I want to talk to you, that's all. Let's sit down."

"Do you want some coffee?"

"Sure." He followed her into the kitchen and while she bustled around making the coffee, he took the time to organize his thoughts.

When she put his perfectly prepared brew in front of him and a plate of her homemade peanut butter cookies between them, he said, "I've been thinking a lot about Dad lately. Maybe because I'm in the same field. Mom, he worked for the force for thirty years and he barely rose in the ranks. But he was our hero at home. You always made us feel that not getting ahead was more noble than, I don't know, being ambitious."

She took a slow sip of her coffee. Put the mug down on the table. Then she raised her gaze and said, "Your father is a wonderful man."

"I know."

"And I love him very much."

"Know that, too."

"He was the kind of police officer who is the real backbone of the force. Loyal, brave, decent and honest. There should be more like him."

He nodded.

"However, fairly early in our marriage I began to see other men being promoted. Smarter men, more political, more ambitious, better educated and better connected perhaps, but they moved up in the ranks and your father barely made lieutenant by the time he retired. I have spent my life supporting him emotionally and reassuring him that I think he's wonderful exactly as he is."

"Do you think I'm getting above myself?" He thought of his recent promotion to detective. How he'd liked not only the raise in pay grade but also the knowledge that he was doing more interesting work. He was beginning to realize that part of his ambivalence about success was rooted in guilt over getting ahead of his father.

His mother looked genuinely stunned by the question. "Why would I think you're getting ahead of yourself? I could not be more proud of you."

"But you always put me down and pump up Dad." He realized how childish he sounded the second the words left his mouth. His mother didn't call him on it, though.

Merely frowned while fiddling with the handle of her mug, as though she were trying to bend it to her will.

"But—but you were born a success. You were always the biggest child in the class, the strongest. You were a good student, a talented athlete, popular. I sometimes wonder how Dennis and I ever managed to produce such an amazing son. I suppose I worried that you being such a gifted person would make Dennis feel bad, so perhaps I overcompensated."

She looked so distressed he wanted to comfort her.

"It's okay, Mom. I know you and Dad love me. I've had a great life. But somewhere I got it into my head that it's wrong to have too much success. I think it's been affecting my performance."

She put down her cup sharply.

Drilled him with her Mom gaze, the one that made him feel ashamed of himself even before she told him what he'd done wrong.

"Adam," she said, "you are thirty-five years old. Don't you think it's time you stopped worrying about what your mother says?"

He grinned at her and rose. "Yes, Mom. I do."

And he walked right around the table, hauled her out of her chair and gave her a smacking kiss on the cheek.

"I love you, Mom."

"I love you, too, Adam. So much. Go and be the success you were meant to be."

Somehow Adam knew that his choking problem wasn't going to be automatically solved simply because he understood one aspect of his family dynamic. But he felt in his gut that he was on his way to figuring out how to get comfortable winning hockey games when they mattered most. He suspected he'd need a few more sessions with

Serena for that to happen. Just thinking about her made him relive the passion they'd shared last night.

He needed a few more sessions with her, all right. A lot of sessions, in fact.

They fell into a sort of routine. He'd drive her to work in the morning, walk her to her office in spite of her protests. He'd make sure that Mark was already there and he and the security expert would have a quick handover meeting. Then he'd head to the precinct. At the end of the workday either he picked her up—his preference—or if he was unable to get away, then Mark would drive her home and get her into her apartment. Mark would have stayed with her until Adam arrived but she'd flipped out so badly the one and only time he'd tried it that, reluctantly, they'd agreed that she could remain inside her locked apartment alone.

He didn't like to think of her being there by herself, not when the perp had already breached her locked door once, but he was in a tough spot. He had other cases. Other work. He couldn't shadow Serena 24/7, as much as he'd have liked to. So he tried to get back to her place as quickly as he could when he knew she was alone.

Once there, his anxiety immediately lifted. He trusted his instincts and training. Nobody was going to get to her. Not on his watch.

Most nights they ate dinner together. Neither one was a gourmet cook, and she preferred a healthy low-fat meal while he was more into throwing a big juicy steak on the grill, teaming it with a fully loaded baked potato and maybe some mushrooms fried in butter to add a vegetable.

However, he'd discovered she wasn't a purist by any means. If he'd suspected she'd eaten pizza with extra cheese at his place only because she'd been traumatized, he soon discovered his mistake. Serena Long ate healthy because it was, well, healthy. But in her heart of hearts, she was a big-plate-dinner kind of gal.

In the interests of balance, he'd agreed to let half of the meals they shared be as healthy as Serena desired while she agreed to spend the other half pigging out with him. Perhaps their meal plan was unorthodox, but so was the entire arrangement they had going, and it was working.

Especially at night when they moved on from sharing a meal to sharing a bed. He'd been blown away by her wild sexiness their first time together and none of their subsequent encounters had changed his opinion. The woman was cool on the outside and molten sex on the inside. An irresistible combination.

The downside, if you could call it that, to all this togetherness was that their stalker had gone silent.

Not a note left at her residence, not a text, not so much as an email. It was as though the man had vanished.

Tonight's routine was no different from that of the past couple of weeks. When Mark brought her home, Adam was already there. The two men nodded at each other. "Anything?" Adam asked.

"Not a thing," Mark replied.

"Okay. See you tomorrow."

When the other man had left, Serena stomped into the kitchen, her eyes snapping, her expression stormy. "What are you doing?"

"Making a salad. I figured I owed you for the chicken and ribs I brought home the other night." They'd been so greasy even he couldn't finish them.

"I don't want salad." She scowled.

"Okay." He had no idea what had got her panties in a twist but he decided to keep cool and hope he figured it out soon. "We'll do something else. Get some takeout."

"I don't want something else. I don't want takeout."

"You want some wine?"

"No! I don't want wine. I want my life back."

She continued to scowl. He continued making salad. "I am being completely unreasonable. Just so we're clear, I am perfectly aware that I'm being a bitch." She glared at him. "Deal with it." She stomped back out of the kitchen and he heard her moving around, muttering to herself.

Deal with it? How, exactly, was he supposed to do that?

He went back to chopping cucumber. At least the mindless task gave him something to do and a reason to stay in the kitchen. If she wanted to seek him out or avoid him, she knew where he was.

He'd purchased a fillet of salmon at the market on his way home and decided to go ahead and grill it in her fancy oven. Maybe when she calmed down she'd want some.

After a while she came back into the kitchen wearing a pair of faded jeans and a white T-shirt. She'd pulled her dark hair back into a ponytail and put fuzzy slippers on her feet.

He glanced at her warily.

She pulled up one of the designer kitchen stools at her granite breakfast bar. Leaned over and filched a chunk of cucumber from off the top of the salad.

"Nothing's happening, Adam. In two weeks nothing has happened. I'm tired of feeling a sick kind of dread every time I check my email and text messages. And then when there's nothing, I feel a perverse annoyance. What is the point of all this security if the guy's moved on to someone else or started taking his meds again or is in jail or something."

"We're being careful."

"I am sick of careful. I feel like you and Mark are following me all the time. I have no privacy, no life of my own. I'm sick of reporting to you on all my movements and having either you or Mark go with me whenever I'm not locked up at home or secreted in my office. I'm starting to feel like you two are the ones stalking me."

He raised his brows at her.

She grabbed a cherry tomato off the counter and popped it in her mouth. "And yes, I know how nuts that sounds. This whole thing is making me nuts."

"Let's give it another week," he said. "If nothing happens in seven more days, then we'll reevaluate."

"Seven days is a long time."

"It's seven nights of hot sex with a partner who can't even watch you steal tomatoes without getting hard."

She snorted with laughter, as he'd hoped she would, then reached for a tomato and, holding his gaze with her own, sucked the red globe into her mouth.

He'd only been kidding about getting hard. Now the joke was on him. He was harder than that cucumber.

Did she think she was the only one who hated this? This waiting? She might think her stalker had moved away or lost interest but Adam did not share that belief. He was certain the guy was playing with them. Lulling them into a false sense of security. He must know by now that she had protection both at home and at work. Perhaps he was planning to wait them out. Wait until Adam and Mark had moved on. And then he'd pounce.

But Adam did not intend for that to happen.

He had a very personal interest in making sure that Serena was safe.

Even with the combined resources of the cops and Max's security firm trying to track him down, the stalker was as elusive as a puff of smoke. As Adam had suspected, the emails were untraceable. The text messages had come from the type of phone popular with drug dealers. It was cheap and, with the addition of an over-the-counter calling card, could be used once and then tossed.

Whoever was behind the harassment was not only crazed but also smart and careful. Adam didn't like the combination.

And he didn't like waiting, waiting for the guy to make the next move.

16

"HOW IS MARCUS DOING?" Serena asked Lisa as their work-day was drawing to a close.

"He's doing really well. He's going to Toastmasters."

Serena blinked. "Are you kidding me?"

"No." Lisa was clearly proud of her client—and her-self. And rightfully so. Serena couldn't believe how well it was working out having Lisa on board as a junior partner. Very soon they were going to have to hire another admin assistant so that Lisa could take on more clients and have more flexibility to get out of the office.

"How did you convince the world's most fearful public speaker to join Toastmasters?"

"I enrolled both of us. And because Marcus wants to be with me all the time, he has to come to the meetings. He can talk for a whole minute without sweating. He's getting there."

Serena chuckled. "Well, it's unorthodox, but whatever works, so long as you don't plan to date all your clients."

Lisa blushed lightly. "No. Only Marcus. He's… Well, he's pretty special. Once you get past the introvert issue, he's fascinating. A gaming genius, obviously. He knows a ton about history and mythology and he's really interested in psychology. He's a Freudian and I'm more of a Jungian, so we never run out of things to talk about."

"And—" Serena glanced out her door to make sure there was no one in earshot and dropped her voice even though Mark was too far away to hear. "I shouldn't even ask, but the sex?"

Lisa's tiny satisfied smile told her everything she needed to know. "Let's just say there's something about a man who's spent his whole life playing games."

She chuckled. "Um, speaking of games, do you know anything about being a dominatrix?"

"Not those kind of games."

"Oh, no, not for you. For me."

Lisa blinked at her. "You want to be a domme?"

"Not for real. It's a kind of a gift to Adam. I've been a little snarly and unreasonable lately. I feel like doing something nice for him."

Lisa was looking at her as though she'd completely lost her mind. "You're going to show your appreciation to Adam by tying him up and spanking him?"

"I feel like there must be more to the dominatrix gig than that. But yes, sort of. He told me that when we first met I reminded him of a dominatrix he once arrested. Turned out they sort of worked together. The way he talked about her I got the feeling it's a bit of a secret fantasy of his. But obviously I don't want to hurt him." She shuddered.

"I'd be more scared of laughing."

"I know. That too."

"Well, I think there are a lot of female characters in gaming who are pretty much dommes. Must be a common male fantasy. You could use them for inspiration. They dress sexy and act all tough and badassy. I think it's about confidence."

"Good point. Thanks."

Lisa gathered her things. "Well, good luck tonight," she said as she left.

"Thanks," Serena replied absently. She was already looking up *dominatrix* on Google. And trying to figure out how she was going to explain their shopping stop on the way home to Mark.

"WHAT DID YOU do today?" Adam asked when Serena showed up at his place after work. They'd started switching nights between his place and hers. He liked having time in his own house, and he thought getting a break from her own space was good for Serena. He had his legs stretched out in front of him and was reading the newspaper.

"A little shopping at a specialty mall."

Something about her tone interested him even though she'd used the words *shopping* and *mall* in the same sentence. "Oh, yeah? Where did you go?"

"A sex store."

The newspaper crackled as he snapped it into a rough fold and put it down on the table. "You don't say." He glanced at the bags in her hand, which she was shielding as best she could. "Looks like you got a lot of stuff."

"I did."

He liked the barely suppressed excitement he could feel coming off her. Caught it from her and felt his own body grow excited. "You going to show me what you got?"

She seemed to consider the idea. "Probably."

He narrowed his gaze at her. "And did you remember to buy batteries?"

"No batteries required. That's what I have you for."

He settled back, enjoying himself. "What might a fine

upstanding member of local law enforcement have to do to get a peek at what's in those bags?"

"First he'd have to go into the bedroom and close the blinds. Then, when the room is completely private, he'd turn out all the lights." She ran her fingertips across his chest. She'd had them painted. Bright blood-red and the tips were filed to points. Interesting look. "Then he'd take off all of his clothes, lie down on the bed naked and wait."

She was turning him on all over the place with her sexy commanding tone, the sharp nails now caressing his jaw, the sense he had that she was intensely aroused.

"Oh, he might, might he? And what would his girl be doing while he's getting butt naked all by himself?"

She chuckled, a dark sound. "You'll see."

He had no idea who this woman was in his house but he kind of liked her. Enough to do what she said. He figured whatever she had in mind, being naked for it was going to be a good thing.

He felt a little foolish following instructions in his own home, but he closed the wooden blinds so no crack of light could enter the bedroom. Then he switched off the light on his bedside table. Finally, he stripped off his clothes. He was completely turned on, eagerly anticipating whatever she planned. He was surprised how dark it was in the room. As he lay on his back on the bed, a minute ticked by. Another. He heard rustling noises coming from the living room. A soft curse.

He was so aroused he felt as though the air had texture, as if it were touching his naked body. He thought about yelling to her to hurry up but decided she'd only go slower if he signaled how impatient he was. Instead he imagined all the things he planned to do to Serena when he got her here beside him, as naked as he was.

He wondered what she'd purchased at the sex store.

Pictured red lace or maybe silk since Serena was always classy. Maybe some massage oil. When he thought about how her hands would feel on his body all slick and slippery, he nearly groaned.

At last the door opened. Of course, since she'd made him turn out the light, he couldn't see a damn thing except the silhouette of her body, dark and somehow mysterious in the doorway. "Did you do as I asked?"

"I'm naked. Yeah. Get in here."

She backed up slightly and brought her right hand into view. It held a lit candle and when his eyes grew accustomed to the brightness, they nearly fell out of his head.

"Serena?" he gasped. She looked amazing. Her hair was held back in a bun, her makeup heavy on the eyes and her lips a deep red. She wore a black PVC corset that barely contained the rise and swell of her breasts. Black fishnet stockings and high-heeled black boots that could stomp him into oblivion.

In the noncandle hand she held a whip. An actual whip. And a black bag that rattled when she moved forward toward the bed.

"You can call me Madame S."

He swallowed. Of course, he had no intention of letting her touch him with that whip but he liked the sexual power he could feel coming off her. He suspected she was enjoying herself.

She put the candle on the bedside table and her black bag of tricks beside it. Those red-tipped hands dipped into the bag and he couldn't help but stare, wondering what would emerge.

A black blindfold.

Black leather restraints.

He glanced up at her. Her dark eyes gleamed. "What are you planning to do with those?"

She shook her head. Made a little tsking sound. "So many questions."

And he had to admit they were stupid ones. What did he think she was planning to do with handcuffs and a blindfold? The whip he was almost positive was merely a prop.

Almost.

The only question for him was, was he going to let her tie him up and blindfold him?

She came closer. Above her stockings were smooth white bands of skin and no panties between him and paradise. "Well?" she asked.

"Well, what?"

"Are you going to submit? Are you going to give up control?"

Of course, they'd been battling over control one way or another pretty much since the day they'd met. But it was one thing to take her advice in coaching sessions. Quite another to let her take the use of his eyes and hands away during sex. While she had hold of a whip. And who knew what was in that bag?

He thought about bargaining. Going for, say, the blindfold but keeping his hands free. But when he looked at her, he saw that this was hard for her and if he refused, she'd probably feel foolish.

Besides, she trusted him every day. Could he not trust her with a little sexual submission?

For answer he raised his hands and wrapped them around the posts of his headboard.

He thought she sighed in relief but he couldn't be certain. Her face gave nothing away.

In the flickering candlelight she leaned over him so her luscious breasts almost rubbed against his chest. She took one of the restraints—it fastened with Velcro, he noted—and wrapped it around his wrist and the bedpost.

He had to force himself not to resist when she tied the second wrist. It might be only Velcro holding him down but he knew it would be a bitch to break the restraints.

"Do you feel helpless?" she asked, clearly reading his mind.

"Yes."

Her red lips curved. "Good."

She lifted the blindfold and he thought to himself that it would be a tragedy if she took his sight away before he got his fill of looking at the sexiest dominatrix he'd ever imagined.

She obviously felt the same, for she merely laid the blindfold over his mouth. He could talk if he wanted to or shake the thing off, but he didn't.

He watched her.

She rose. Picked up the whip. He didn't like where this seemed to be going. He was naked, vulnerable and faceup!

"I could do anything to you. You know that, don't you?"

He nodded.

She touched the whip to his chest where his heart beat, then traced it slowly down his body. When she got to his crotch, his penis twitched.

She smiled. Took the end of the lash and wound it around his cock slowly. The combination of her fingers stroking and the leather winding was incredible, delicious torture. He nearly burst right then. As though sensing how close to the boiling point he was, she unwound the leather and placed the whip on the bed.

Now she stood and lifted the blindfold off his mouth, then carefully placed it over his eyes. Lifting his head with one hand, she looped the strap behind.

Now he was blind and tied up.

What had he allowed?

He felt her move beside him, heard more rattling and assumed she was once more delving into the black bag.

For what?

He felt her hands on his chest. First she ran her open palms down his torso. Then he felt the scratch of her nails follow the path. Not hard—it was a scrape that he could only hear in his sightless state. And he could see those red-tipped sharp nails skim down his body in his imagination as clearly as though he were watching.

The sensations were electric.

"Spread your legs," she ordered.

To his amazement he complied. He realized that about now she could tell him to do anything and he'd do it. Beg, bark like a dog, kiss her feet, anything if only she'd quit torturing him and do something with the raging erection that was becoming almost painful.

"Good," she said.

Once more he heard the rattling sound. This time he felt a shock of cold on his chest. Took him a second to recognize that she was tracking a piece of ice down the center of his chest. He was so hot that the thing was nothing but a puddle by the time she got to his navel.

More rattling. A new piece of ice. She picked up where the other one had melted. Down below his navel. Lower.

And then she stopped.

More rattling.

He felt her lips on his cock. Cool lips, slick with gloss. And then she opened on him and he gasped. His hips bucked.

17

HER MOUTH WAS filled with ice water. And chunks of ice, he realized as she moved her mouth up and down on him.

Cold rivulets were running down his cock, and yet there were hints of heat in her mouth. He could barely stand it.

Then, when he was sure he'd die on the spot, she pulled away.

He felt movement on the bed as though she was climbing onto it. Oh, yes, her knee brushed his belly as she straddled him.

"You know what I learned today about dommes?" she asked softly. He couldn't form words, never mind think. He grunted.

"I learned that a professional dominatrix doesn't have sex with her clients." She hovered over him, so close he could feel her warm, slick heat.

She waited for him to get her meaning and groan helplessly.

"Good thing I'm not a professional," she said, and drove her hot, wet luscious body down onto him.

Hot, sweet, tight. Oh, he couldn't hold on. He couldn't.

She rode him and he bucked beneath her, wishing he had his hands free to hold her, wishing he had his eyes free to watch her eyes cloud over and her head fall back the way it did when she came.

But he couldn't do either of those things; he could only thrust up and up, wild with need. She was as wild as he, her hips gyrating madly as she took him deep within her body. He heard her moan and then he felt her body clench around him as her climax hit.

It was all he needed to burst his dam.

With a surge, he thrust up and up, crying hoarsely his release.

"UM, DO YOU THINK you could untie me now?"

She sat back on her heels and regarded him. At least she'd removed the blindfold. But she seemed uncertain about taking off the restraints. "I don't know. I kind of like you like this. Powerless. In my complete control."

"I promise that you can do that to me anytime," he said. "You don't need to tie me down. I'll go willingly."

"It's more fun when you're tied up."

"Well, how 'bout we change spots and I'll tie you up?"

"Nice try. A dom/sub relationship only goes one way."

He had a bad feeling he'd been way too quick to let her take control. Seemed she wasn't in a "first you, now me" kind of mood. Which he might be okay with if she'd hurry up and untie his hands.

He thought about it for a minute. "You know, if I had my hands free, there are so many ways I could please you, Madame S."

"You do have a point," she agreed, and finally leaned over and unfastened the restraints. He waited until she had the second one off, waited until she'd stopped looking at him with suspicion.

Then he pounced.

She shrieked, laughing as he grabbed her wrists and

pinned them with his hands. "Not fair," she cried, trying
to wiggle out from under him, which only served to get
him all excited again.

From the way she was beginning to breathe heavily he
suspected she was getting worked up again too.

"Control," he informed her, sucking one plump nipple
into his mouth and nipping it gently, "is more fun when
it's shared." She sighed and arched her back as he went
for the second one.

"Agreed."

SERENA FELT A tenderness between her legs as she worked
out on the elliptical the next morning. As she got the machine really moving, she also felt the tenderness in her
nipples where Adam had tormented them yesterday. She
couldn't believe the intensity of the sex they'd experienced.
She was letting herself go in ways she'd never have believed she was capable of. It wasn't that she was a prude.
She'd been in sex stores before, purchased the odd discreet toy, but to get herself rigged out as a dominatrix and
take complete control of her lover's body was something
completely new.

He'd loved it.

Amazingly, so had she.

Games. She seemed to be surrounded by them. Hockey
games as the Hunter Hurricanes did their best to dominate
league play; video games, which were serious business to
Marcus Lemming and her new junior partner, Lisa. And
now sex games between her and Adam. Which, now she
came to think about it, were also serious stuff in some
ways. It seemed as though in order for her to let go like that
in sex play she had to trust in a way she never had before.

What did that mean?

When you opened up to a man like that? Trusted him

body and soul. Allowed yourself to be completely vulnerable.

She nearly tripped herself on the workout apparatus as the obvious answer hit her.

She was in love.

In love with Adam.

"Are you all right?" a man's voice asked from the machine beside hers. "You sounded like my dog does after he eats one of my socks."

"Yes," she said, finding her rhythm once again. "I just had a…choking thing."

"Sure. Glad I don't need to dust off my CPR skills."

It occurred to her that this man was using Stan's machine and had been for a few days now. "Where's Stan?" she asked, then felt stupid because why would this man have a clue who Stan was?

"Stan Wozniak?" Okay, he had a clue.

"Yes."

"He went to Poland to visit his mother and sisters."

"Stan's in Poland?" She'd been so caught up in her own affairs she hadn't been coming to the gym regularly. Hadn't even realized that Stan wasn't there, either.

"Yeah. I think he gets back tomorrow. This is usually his machine. I use that one in the corner. But the view's better here. You can see out the window."

"I know. That's why I like this machine."

"Maybe I'll start getting here five minutes before Stan from now on." He grabbed his towel and wiped sweat from his neck. "You snooze, you lose."

Even through a busier-than-usual day, she felt a vague niggle of discomfort. Stan was away. The messages had stopped.

Stan was coming back tomorrow.

When Mark dropped her off at Adam's place, she found

him shoving a freshly washed jersey into his hockey bag. "Hey," he said, "I ate without you. There's pizza in the box."

"Okay," she said. She gave him a quick kiss, changed into black jeans and a black T-shirt. Washed up and grabbed a slice of pizza. She spread open the newspaper he'd obviously been reading earlier. "What time's your game?"

"Nine-fifteen. It's only forty-five minutes long. Come and cheer the team," he said. "Be a supportive girlfriend."

"I'm not your girlfriend," she snapped. Since she'd realized she was in love with him, everything had felt strange.

He seemed unfazed by having his head snapped off. "Okay. Be a supportive fake girlfriend. It'll be fun. And you can meet my parents."

"Meet your parents?"

"Yeah. Ever since Mom and I had our talk, she's been trying to get to a few games. You know, be supportive. Cheer in an embarrassingly loud voice."

He made it sound foolish but she knew how important this was for him. And she liked his mother instinctively for so quickly trying to change her behavior. She felt cranky and emotionally vulnerable now that she knew she was in love with Adam, but she also wanted to spend as much time as she could with the guy since she was sure he'd be gone as soon as her case was closed. Which she suspected was imminent. "Okay, I'll come."

She didn't want to mess up his concentration but she knew she had to tell him about Stanley. So she did on the way to the rink.

Adam didn't react as strongly as she'd imagined he would. "So he gets back tomorrow?"

"That's what Gary thinks. Gary's the man who was working out beside me today."

"Maybe don't go to the gym for a couple of days. Let's hope Stanley got laid in Poland and has a new crush."

"So you don't think it's him?"

"It could be Stanley. Could also be a list of other people. The important thing is to be ready for anything and to keep you safe."

She reached for his hand. "And to have fun tonight."

In the sportsplex where the Hurricanes played, there were eight rinks. Upstairs was a bar and snack shop surrounded by huge walls of glass so spectators could view the action on all the rinks in comfort. When Adam headed to the dressing room, she ran upstairs to the snack bar and bought herself a hot chocolate.

Banners hung over the rinks celebrating various victories over the years. In one rink she watched young women play hockey. A few had bright pink helmets on and many a ponytail hung down over the back of a jersey.

On the next rink over figure skaters practiced. All loops and jumps and a pair of ice dancers waltzing.

Next to that was, strangely, an indoor soccer game. Instead of ice, the playing surface was turf.

She ran back downstairs because she preferred to be closer to the action. Closer to Adam. She sat in the bleachers and was soon joined by an older couple. The man looked so much like an older version of Adam that she smiled at them and the woman took the man's hand and brought him over. They sat beside her. "I'm Adam's mother, June. And this is Dennis."

She shook both their hands. "I'm so glad to meet you. I'm Serena."

"I thought you must be. You're wearing Adam's jacket."

She laughed. "I am." The down jacket was far too big but much warmer than anything she owned.

She liked his parents immediately. They were comfortable people. Easy to talk to. Nice. When the teams filed in, there weren't many people watching. The three of them, a couple of young guys and two women in hockey gear who seemed to be sitting down for a rest after their own game.

When play started, Serena quickly got caught up in the game. So close to the action, she could hear the bang of skates on boards, bodies on boards, the crunching slide of skates on ice and the constant back-and-forth between players.

"Open, open, open," one would yell.

"Here, here, here," another would cry. She wondered how the guys managed to keep track of where everyone was. She could barely keep track of one man. Adam was number 10. When he was on the ice, she had eyes for no one else. He scored the first goal, which meant a great deal of loud and embarrassing cheering from his three supporters.

When the game was over, a sweaty Adam came over to his cheering section. "Hi, Mom, Dad," he said.

"You were terrific, honey," his mother gushed.

"Nice play, son."

"Thanks. You met Serena?"

"Of course."

"Listen, can you stay with her while I grab a quick shower? I'll be back in ten."

"Of course, dear."

He didn't stop to hear her argue that she was perfectly safe in a public sports complex for ten minutes.

When they got back to his place, she tried to tell him as much but then he started kissing her and she lost her train of thought.

18

ADAM SEEMED TO have a smile perma-glued to his face. Great sex with an amazing woman could do that to a man. His partner only seemed more miserable than usual. "Stop sounding so happy," Joey snapped as he drove them toward the docks where a container ship was being held up for containing suspicious cargo.

"What?" He was sitting minding his own business, reliving some choice moments with Serena in the privacy of his own head. What was Virge's problem?

"You're whistling."

He was? "I was?"

"Yeah. You're not a whistler. You start that up and I'll have to get a new partner."

They'd been partners for more than a year. Adam had no wish to break in somebody new. "Sorry. I'll stick to morose silence so you feel at home."

"Thank you."

They drove on in silence. Maybe Adam was banned from whistling but not even Joey the Virgin could stop the direction of his thoughts. Joey'd whistle, too, if he had a storehouse of recent memories like Adam's. He'd sing arias if he had the images Adam did crowding his head. Serena in nothing but stilettos and fishnets.

Serena, her eyes clouding over and tiny cries emerging from her luscious mouth as he drove her to her peak. Serena, sleeping beside him, her hair spilling onto his shoulder. Her face unguarded in sleep. He'd only known her a few weeks, and now he couldn't imagine her not being in his life.

The streets rolled past and he forced himself to start focusing on the day's task. "What do we know about the container ship?" he asked Joey.

"Not much. Suspicious cargo. What the hell does that mean? It's drugs? Stolen cars? Stowaways?" He shook his head. "Probably get taken away from us anyway if it's anything good." Joey was still irritable that the DEA had claimed jurisdiction of the grow-op investigation when it turned out to be part of a much larger network.

Adam would normally be more keen to tackle a big case, but right now he didn't want to be involved in anything that would involve a lot of overtime. He needed to be around for Serena.

They stopped to grab a takeout coffee on the way. "You can buy, Mr. Happy," Joey said, pulling over.

It was his turn anyway, so he merely grunted and dashed into the corner coffee place for two takeouts. When he got back to the car, Joey pulled a U-turn the second he was inside the car.

"What's going on?"

"The container ship will have to wait." He sounded keyed up, as if something big was happening.

"Why?"

"Suspicious death," Joey said. "Downtown. Just got called in."

"What do we know?" The crime rate in Hunter, Washington, wasn't very high. Murder was extremely rare. Suspicious death usually meant somebody didn't die of old age in their bed or of a known illness in hospital.

"Female. Found in the lobby of an apartment building. Tenant found her. Had the sense not to move her."

An awful sense of dread crept over Adam's skin. "What's the address?"

Joey told him. It was Serena's building.

He didn't say a word, but every fiber of his being shouted, *No! Not Serena.*

Maybe she wasn't dead. Joey had said no one had touched the body. It could be another game. Maybe the perp had just knocked Serena out, not killed her.

Adam had to believe that. He had to hang on.

It took all his self-control not to scream at Joey to drive faster. The guy was going as fast as he could.

When they drew closer to the building, he snapped, "Go left down the next lane. It's faster." He knew this area well because he'd driven it a lot lately and he'd mapped out the area in his mind in case he ever needed to get to Serena fast. Or get her away from the area in haste.

Never had he anticipated this scenario. He refused to let himself imagine the worst. They were almost there.

Joey pulled up in front of the building with a screech of tires. A couple of uniforms were already there.

Adam didn't wait for Joey to turn off the engine. He was out of the car and racing for the building.

A uniform opened it for him. "Haven't touched anything. Witness who called it in is over there. Body's this way."

He led Adam around the corner to the trio of elevators. Their shoes clipped against the marble lobby floor. A churchlike hush enveloped the place. Even though there were probably a dozen people hanging around watching, no one spoke.

Adam slipped on surgical gloves. Had trouble because his hands wouldn't stay steady.

She lay facedown. A spill of black hair draped over her face like a shroud. She wore a black skirt and a blue sweater. One high heel had fallen off and lay beside her on the floor.

Adam wasn't a praying man, but right now he wished he were. Wished he could beg for Serena to be alive. He'd do anything, give up his own life if it would preserve hers. Because a world without Serena wasn't a world he cared to live in.

He knelt. Pressed two fingers to her carotid artery. No pulse. Her skin was as cold as the marble she lay on. Even before he'd touched her he'd known she was dead. There was a stillness about the body he recognized. The stillness of death.

He felt a kind of fog come over him. He knew he'd face the full impact of his pain soon enough, but for now the fog helped keep him from experiencing the full horror of the moment.

Gently, he brushed the hair back to reveal her face.

A stranger's face.

THE RELIEF ADAM felt was so intense he was glad he was down on his haunches. He wavered and his gaze went blank. In that moment Adam knew. He was in love with Serena. A love so intense that the thought of life without her was impossible to contemplate.

He rose slowly.

Joey stood back regarding the scene.

He removed the gloves. Walked forward. "She's dead, all right."

"You okay?" his partner asked.

He nodded briefly. "This is Serena's building. Dead woman looks like her from the back."

Joey blew out a breath as the obvious implication hit. He'd been involved in her case in a peripheral way but he had to know that Adam wasn't simply a cop doing his job where Serena was concerned. His involvement was as personal as it gets. "You think there could be a connection?"

Adam had a really bad feeling that there was. "I don't know, but I don't like it. Seems like a pretty big coincidence. Let's talk to the woman who found the victim. Then I'm going to see Serena."

They walked over to an older woman sitting in a lobby chair. She had the stunned look he'd come to associate with the loved ones of violent-crime victims and those who stumble on death unexpectedly.

The uniformed cop had given Adam a brief history. The woman's name was Eleanor McCormack. She was a retired history teacher. She'd been on her way out to get groceries when she stumbled on the crime scene. Adam approached the woman. "Hi, Mrs. McCormack. I'm Detective Shawnigan. This is Detective Sorento."

"Hello," she said. Polite. A vinyl shopping bag on wheels, empty, sat at her feet. Her wool coat was still buttoned, ready to go out. A poodle brooch set with fake diamonds was pinned to her collar.

"Mind if we ask you a few questions?"

"No. Of course not."

He took the chair beside her. Joey pulled a third chair around so they were sitting in a ragged circle.

"This was quite a shock for you. Can you tell us what happened?"

"Well, I was on my way out to do some shopping. Percy—that's my dog—is out of Milk-Bones. And I need some milk and bread. Things like that." She clasped her hands together.

"Did you take the elevator down to the lobby or the stairs?"

"The elevator. I live on the fifth floor."

Joey had his notebook out, but Adam simply concentrated on Mrs. McCormack's words.

"I came out of the elevator and—and there she was. The poor woman. Lying there on the floor. I didn't know what to do. I called out, 'Are you all right?' but she didn't answer. I was alarmed, of course. I didn't know what to do. Oh, I already said that. Well, I simply didn't. I think I knew she was dead, but I wouldn't want to make assumptions if a life could be saved. I have my CPR, you know, from when I used to volunteer at the Shakespeare festival. Anyway—" Eleanor McCormack's hand fluttered to her chest and he saw that it was shaking "—I checked her pulse, but there wasn't one."

"What time was this?"

"Not very long ago. I watched *Good Morning America* and as soon as it was over, I brushed my teeth and put on my coat. Say five minutes after that I came down. I called 911 as soon as I'd checked her pulse. It's a good thing I remembered my cell phone. Usually I forget to unplug it from the wall, but my children insist I take it with me wherever I go. Silly, really. What did they think we did for all those years there weren't any such thing as cell phones? Anyway, now I make sure I always have my phone in my purse when I go out." She clutched the worn black leather bag in her lap. She seemed to realize she was rambling and stopped herself with an effort. "I called right after I checked that poor girl's pulse."

"Did you see anyone?"

"No. It was just me."

"No one in the lobby? Just leaving?"

She shook her head.

"Did you hear the elevator?"

"Not that I can recall."

Adam had a mental snapshot of the scene in his mind. He glanced at Mrs. McCormack's purse and her bag. Realized the dead woman had nothing in her hands or around her.

"A few minutes later a couple came in the front door." She gestured with her chin. "That's them over there. Ghouls. Then I called the building supervisor. And the police came quite quickly. And a few other people have come out of the elevator or in from the street."

"Do you recognize the dead woman?"

"I can't tell. Her face was obscured by her hair. But I don't think so."

"Did you notice a purse or bag of any kind? When you discovered her?"

"I didn't really pay attention. But I didn't notice one."

"Thank you. You've been very helpful. You can go now."

Mrs. McCormack rose slowly. Glanced in the direction of the dead woman. "She seems so young. Do you suppose it was a heart attack?"

"Impossible to tell until the medical examiner gets here. You absolutely did the right thing in calling us right away and not trying to move her."

A police photographer showed up while they were interviewing Mrs. McCormack and began snapping photos. The medical examiner and the forensic guys were right behind him.

Adam and Joey watched and waited. Joey said, "What do you think happened to her purse? Some guy hit her on the head and stole it?"

"Inside her building lobby?"

"Maybe she doesn't carry one."

"Then where's her cell phone? Building key?"

"Maybe she's lying on them."

But when they flipped the body, there was nothing underneath her. And her skirt had pockets. When they first turned her, Adam saw a flash of red and thought for a moment the dead woman's throat had been slit. Then his vision cleared and he realized she had a red scarf tied around her neck.

And any faint hope he'd harbored that this death was completely unrelated to Serena died a fast death.

In a few minutes the medical examiner came over to them, a portly man in his fifties. "What do you think, Doc?" Joey asked.

"Hard to tell. She's got a bump on her head. That's the only sign of trauma I can see. But she could have hit her head on the way down. Could be heart, an aneurism. Severe allergic reaction to something. I'll let you know the autopsy results as soon as I can."

"Could it be murder?"

He shrugged. A man who'd seen death in a hundred forms. "No signs of struggle or foul play. But anything's possible."

They began bagging the body and Adam turned away.

To Joey he said, "It's murder, all right. That scarf around her neck? It's like the red crayon blood Serena's stalker drew on the happy face he scrawled. The perp killed that woman and planted the body here. I'm sure of it. He's sending a message."

Joey glanced at the body bag and back to Adam. "Pretty dramatic message."

"Yeah." He grabbed his cell phone and called Serena immediately.

"Hi, Adam," she answered, sounding happy to hear from him.

"Where are you?"

"I'm at the office." Obviously she heard the tension in his voice. "Is everything all right?"

"No. Stay where you are. I'm on my way. Do not let anyone in that office."

"All right, but I wish you'd tell me—"

He disconnected. Called Mark. "You're in lockdown. Lock the office. Nobody comes near Serena until I get there. Got that?"

"Affirmative."

SERENA TRIED NOT to panic, but each minute that passed as she waited for Adam to arrive seemed like an ice age. The tone of his voice told her something seriously bad had happened.

Her stomach felt jumpy and she couldn't settle. Mark locked the front door. Drew his weapon. Put Lisa and her together in her office. Told her to lock her office door.

"What do you think happened?" Lisa asked.

"I don't know. This is the worst part, the waiting, not knowing anything." She couldn't work, couldn't sit, couldn't do anything but pace. Lisa sat in a chair, staring at the glass sculpture. She took a tissue from the box on Serena's desk and began dusting the colorful glass, obsessively, focused completely on her task, while Serena paced, rubbing cold hands up and down her upper arms as though she could soothe herself.

Fortunately, they didn't have long to wait.

Adam shouted at her to open her door and she did. He looked as though he'd aged ten years and did something he'd never done before in front of Lisa and Mark.

He pulled her into his arms. Kissed her. She felt tension in every cell of his body. He squeezed her so tight she could barely breathe. She realized he was shaking.

When she pulled away, she asked, "What? What is going on?"

Adam's partner, Joey, stood behind him. Impassive and dejected looking. But then, according to Adam, Joey always looked dejected.

"Sit down. You too, Mark. Joey will take over watch."

With a nod, Joey moved to the front office.

Mark and Lisa sat. She couldn't. So she stood by the window and watched Adam. He said, "We had a call this morning. A woman was found dead in the lobby of your apartment building."

Her eyes widened. "Oh, how awful. Was it someone I know?"

He drilled her with his gaze. "Don't have an ID yet. She had nothing on her. She looked a lot like you. She was facedown in the lobby of your apartment building."

Her hand drifted to her throat. "How did she die?"

His gaze went to where her hand rested. She could feel her pulse jump. "Blow to the head. Could have been accidental, but I don't think so. I think she was murdered."

"No." She didn't realize she'd said the word aloud until she heard it. More like a moan than an actual word. "Oh, no."

"She had a red scarf tied around her neck."

"A lot of people wear scarves," Mark said in his soft voice.

"Yeah. But the guy sending the messages left Serena a picture of a smiley face with blood coming out of its mouth."

"Do you think the killer hit the wrong woman? A case of mistaken identity?" Mark asked, crisp and professional.

"Could be. We'll know more when we discover her

identity and whether she lives in the building. But my gut says it's the guy who's been sending those messages. He chose a woman who looks like Serena deliberately. He's letting Serena know he's coming for her." His words were cold, brutal. He sounded angry.

"But why would anyone kill an innocent woman to send me a message?"

Adam turned to her. Eyes blazing. "Because he's a sick bastard who gets his thrills from tormenting you. He's leading up to the big finale in his game."

"You mean, he's planning—"

He grabbed her arms, blue eyes burning into hers. "He can plan all he wants. He's not getting you."

There was silence for several seconds. Then Lisa said, "But there's been nothing for two weeks. Now, suddenly, he does this? Why now? What's different?"

Serena and Adam exchanged glances.

"Stanley," she said.

"Stanley?" Lisa echoed. "The guy at the gym?"

"I was working out the day before yesterday and noticed that Stanley wasn't using the machine beside mine. It was another man. An older guy. He works out around the same time, too. We got chatting and he mentioned that Stanley was in Poland visiting family." She could hardly stand to spit out the next part. "Stanley was due back yesterday."

19

"CAN YOU LEAVE NOW?" Adam asked. He couldn't stand the thought of Serena being vulnerable and him not being right there to protect her.

She nodded. "It's not like I'll get any work done." She turned to her assistant. "Lisa, we might as well lock up for the day."

"I've got work, and Marcus scheduled a meeting."

"Go to his work. Or reschedule. I don't want you here on your own."

He saw Lisa give a slight shudder. "I'll get hold of Marcus."

Then Adam took Serena home. There was no discussion. He drove her to his place. She already had an extra toothbrush and some of her things there, enough that she didn't need to stop at her apartment. Even if she'd wanted to go there, he'd have refused. He wasn't remotely surprised that she didn't.

They got to his place and he felt the newfound knowledge that he loved her burn deep within him. It wasn't a happy, contented sort of love. Not today. His feelings were more like a fiery need to keep her safe, to protect her from any harm and to pulverize anybody or anything that threatened.

He suspected he'd slipped right back to some caveman stage of male development and knew he was operating on the most basic of instincts.

When they got to his place, he hustled her inside. Then he turned to her, took her face in his hands and said, "I thought for a second that was you. I—" He hoped she could read his feelings in his eyes, because he couldn't say the words—the emotion was too strong. Instead he pulled her soft, beautiful body against him and kissed her, giving in to his equally primal urge to mate.

When she responded to him, when her lips trembled beneath his and she opened to him, he thought he might have grunted. No time for patience, no time for careful wooing; he needed her so badly he ached. He bent and put an arm under her knees, lifted her into the air and stalked into his bedroom. She made a small sound of surprise when he lifted her, but they never broke the kiss. He managed to flip back the covers before placing her down on the bed.

With his newfound awareness that he loved this woman, he wanted to take things slowly, to seduce her with every part of him until she realized she loved him, too. But his need was too great. He couldn't hold back. And because she shared his urgency, he was lost. They tore at each other's clothes, not even waiting to get naked. He yanked up her skirt, had her hose and panties off in one tug. He heard some soft fabric tear. Meanwhile, she attacked his belt buckle, dragged at his zipper. He helped her yank his slacks down past his knees and didn't bother removing anything else.

He took her as a caveman would. Rough, hard, thrusting, thrusting as though he could reach the very heart of her. She met him with equal force, her hips grinding against him as though she could suck him in and up to the very heart of her.

His climax was a bone-shattering explosion. It was as though a part of him believed that if he could pump all his life force into her, he could somehow keep her safe.

She didn't let him go but kept grinding her hips against him until he felt her inner muscles clench him like a vice. Her head fell back and she cried out. He held her tight through her explosive climax.

Their breathing was harsh in the quiet room and as it slowed, he took stock. The bedding was a tangle, their clothes twisted and pulled all over the place. "Wow," she said in a deeply sated tone.

"I acted like an animal," he said, ashamed of himself. "I didn't even take your clothes off."

She rose over him, kissed him deeply. "Guess you're going to have to start all over again, then."

So he did. Taking the time to undress her slowly, properly. Kissing and caressing her as he did so.

They stopped briefly to raid the fridge around eleven when hunger got in their way. Then they continued making love far into the night.

ADAM REMAINED vigilant, so keyed up he felt as though he were mainlining espresso. He wanted to be with her 24/7 but even if his job would have allowed it, Serena wouldn't. One day bled into the next.

Nothing happened.

The perp didn't make a move of any kind.

"Joey, we need to get a search warrant for Stanley Wozniak's apartment, his place of business. He's our guy. I'm sure of it," he said as they finished up a morning briefing session at the station.

"Why?" Virge wore his long-suffering look.

Adam related the details. The fact that the perp had gone quiet during the exact times Stanley was out of the country. "Then, the second day he's back, he goes crazy and kills a woman who looks like Serena."

"And another week's gone by with nothing."

"It's part of his plan to scare Serena and mess with us."

"What evidence do you have?" Joey asked. "What evidence will convince a judge to let us enter Stanley Wozniak's residence? And to prove what? That he broke into her apartment to leave a tasteless joke?"

"He murdered a woman and left her in Serena's lobby. A woman who looks a lot like Serena."

Joey sighed, the exhausted sigh of a man whose patience was nearing its limit. "We talked to him. He didn't know that girl and his alibi is pretty solid. He came home from Poland and his house was flooded. He was at home with workmen and plumbers, up to his knees in water, when Patricia Hagan died."

"He could have slipped away. No way anyone would have noticed if he was gone for an hour or so. That's all it would have taken. He sneaks away from the crew cleaning up from the flood, kills the girl, dumps her body in the lobby to send Serena another message. Then he goes back to his flooded house."

"And once again, I have to remind you that we don't have any evidence that Miss Hagan was murdered. Death was probably accidental."

"A blow to the head killed her. Otherwise she was a healthy twenty-nine-year-old."

"She was also a mountain climber, a cyclist, an athlete. You heard the M.E. She could have cracked her head and not realized she had a concussion. Her brain's bleeding and she doesn't know it. She gets ready to go to work, has a headache, her vision's kind of blurry. She figures it'll pass. She takes the elevator downstairs *because she lives in the building,* gets to the lobby and poof, she's dead." Joey waved his hands around as though he were stage-directing a play.

"Or she was hit on the head from behind by someone who is so familiar with human anatomy they know the exact spot on the skull where one blow can kill a woman. Like, say, someone in the medical field."

"You're stretching."

"Where was her stuff? Her keys? A bag? There was nothing at all on the body. I've been in that building. You need a key fob for just about everything. Yet hers was missing."

Joey shrugged. "I don't know. Maybe she went to check her mail and realized she'd forgotten her key. Turns back to return to her apartment and—"

"Yeah, yeah. Poof, she's dead." He was so frustrated, so edgy he couldn't see straight. "What about the scarf?"

"A popular fashion accessory," Joey said with the infinite patience of a man who's had the same argument too many times.

"It's too much of a coincidence."

"My friend, coincidences happen all the time."

Adam banged his fist against his palm so hard he felt the blow all the way to his elbow. "You don't believe Patty Hagan's death is unrelated to Serena's stalker any more than I do."

"I believe in the due process of law and not going off like a grenade without any proof."

Joey was right, of course. He wanted to kick something. "Come on. Stanley Wozniak's smitten with Serena. Could have swiped her keys from her purse while she was working out, gone to her place. Got the spare set. He knows her routines, where she lives."

"So could any other person who works out at the gym and knows her even slightly. Somebody who's been in her office could also have taken Serena's keys. She's a pretty high-profile person. A lot of people come in contact with her." Joey put his coffee mug on the coaster he kept on his neat desktop. "Seems to me, Stanley Wozniak isn't the only one smitten with Serena. Maybe your personal feelings are screwing with your judgment?"

"But what if I'm right?" He knew his partner had a valid point and that only pissed him off even more. "If Patricia Hagan was murdered, then we both know the murderer is coming for Serena."

"I CAN'T LIVE like this," Serena snapped as she replaced the free weights in the rack with a clack. She and Adam were working out in the gym in her apartment building, which was small, smelled of stale air and sweat, and didn't have an elliptical. "I feel like a prisoner. I want to go to my own gym."

"It's too dangerous."

"But nothing's happened! You got me all worked up and I thought some poor woman was murdered, because of me, but the paper said she was an athlete who probably died from a brain injury suffered doing sports."

"I think your stalker killed her."

"And what if he didn't? What if the sick prankster who sent me those messages has moved on? Then I'm under house arrest for nothing."

"You're not under house arrest. Don't be dramatic." Adam looked overtired. She knew he was barely sleeping. He was so certain that some guy was about to pounce that he had her scared of her own shadow. "You watch me constantly. You control every move I make. I feel stifled and confined."

"Stifled? Confined?" He bellowed the words, disbelief in every line of his body. "Well, that's a hell of a lot better than dead!"

She took a deep breath. "I know. You're right. I am being unreasonable, but it's awful living like this. When you watch me every second as though you're terrified some deranged killer is going to pounce if you take your eyes off me for a second, what do you think that does to me? I can't live in fear. Not anymore. I did that long enough in my life. I won't do it again." She couldn't stand her own feelings of vulnerability. She'd worked so hard to live with confidence and courage and now she was being dragged back to a fear that was all too reminiscent of her childhood.

"It's not going to be forever," he said. "Have patience."

"I'm out of patience."

Adam replaced his own free weights, much larger ones than Serena had used. His gray T-shirt had a sexy sweat stain down the front and clung to his impressive torso. She didn't want to notice, didn't want to be aroused by his nearness. "I admit I'm being overprotective. Believe me, Joey's given me the same lecture. But I can't protect you here. I can't protect you and, at the same time, catch the guy who's stalking you. I need for you to go away somewhere."

"Go away?"

"Yes."

"Where?" Her temper started to build. She had assumed her confinement couldn't get any worse. She had a bodyguard at work, another at home. He'd stopped her going to the gym, the grocery store. He'd even nixed a manicure. Now Adam wanted to send her away?

"I don't know. And I don't care. Somewhere where you'll be safe. Take a vacation. We'll get a police officer to pose as you. Draw the perp out. Then when we've got him, you can come back."

"How long do you think it will take?"

"I don't know. Couple of weeks maybe?"

Her fingers tapped her arm in frustration. "And is your police officer going to give the keynote address to the accountants' association that's been booked for more than two months?"

"I know it's not perfect—"

"And is the police officer going to take my place at all the other events on my calendar? Is she going to see my clients and run my business?"

"Lisa can take up the slack," he said lamely.

"Lisa is learning the business. It's still my business and I need to be here to run it. So thank you for the suggestion, but I'm not going anywhere."

"Quit being so stubborn and unreasonable." She felt his anger blaze into life and it ignited her own.

"Me?" She shrieked the word. "Me? Stubborn and unreasonable? Look in the mirror if you want to see stubborn and unreasonable. And while you're looking, you'll see controlling and dictatorial, too."

"I'm trying to keep you safe." He banged a weight up and back into the rack, and the sound echoed off the walls.

"You're trying to scare me and kill my business. In fact, you're doing the smiley-face guy's work for him."

He grabbed her shoulders, blazing eyes staring into her face. "I can't lose you."

She yanked herself out of his grasp. She felt smothered. She'd let herself fall for him. Become more vulnerable than she'd ever let herself be with a man. And look where it got her. He was sounding as deranged as her stalker. She couldn't stand it. "You are losing me. Right now."

He acted as though she hadn't spoken. "Leave town. I mean it."

"I'm not leaving." She glared at him, knowing she was overreacting and not caring. "You are."

"What?' He seemed genuinely stunned.

"Right now. You're leaving my home. I don't want you here."

"Don't be irrational. You need me."

"No. I don't." She leaned against the wall beside the water station that was, as usual, empty. "I wasn't planning to tell you this but when I called you at the office yesterday, Joey answered your phone. He feels you're losing perspective."

Adam took a swift step back, as though he'd been kicked. "Joey said that?"

"Well, I asked for his honest opinion of the level of risk. He doesn't think I'm in as much danger as you do."

"One man's opinion."

"What about my opinion? Doesn't that count for anything? I need my life. I need my freedom. I've changed my locks. I drive my car to the office and home. I can't stand being watched all day and all night. It's making me crazy."

"Fine." He threw up his hands. "Fine. So you want me to leave? Is that what you want?"

Did she? Her feelings were a mess. When she'd said she was going crazy, she hadn't entirely exaggerated. She was falling for Adam and falling hard. Their sex was so searingly intimate it scared her. Her own feelings confused her. If only she could have some time to herself to think. To sort out her own messed-up psyche.

"I think I do need a short holiday," she said. "I'll be extra careful, but please, could you give me a couple of days to myself?"

He stood for a moment in silence. Then he said, "This

is against every instinct I have as a cop. But if you tell me to leave, I will."

"Thank you."

He stomped out of the gym. She let him go.

She waited a couple of minutes, then took the elevator up to her apartment. When she got into her suite, she was in time to see Adam head out, his bag so swiftly packed a sock hung out of it.

She could see how much he hated to leave her. She didn't like the feeling inside that wanted her to tell him she'd changed her mind, to beg him to stay.

"You see or hear anything, anything at all, you call me."

"I will."

His gaze searched her face, then he kissed her, swift and hard, and she tasted his anger and frustration.

As the door slammed behind him, she slumped down in the nearest chair. She'd just kicked the man she was frighteningly sure she loved out of her apartment.

What had she done?

"LISA? CAN I talk to you?"

"Of course."

Serena had barely slept the night before, after she'd asked Adam to leave, and she knew she needed someone to talk to. Someone she could trust.

"I mean professionally. As a psychologist."

"I'm not licensed, but sure." The nice thing about having Mark around was that he could take over the reception desk when Lisa met with Serena or when she left the office, as she was starting to do again. Serena realized how many things she'd put on hold because of the craziness, but that was over. She was certain that whoever had sent her those crazed messages had lost interest in her. The tragic death of the young woman was an unfortunate accident.

And Serena needed to get her own life back on track. Starting by hiring a new admin assistant next week.

Once Mark was at the front desk and Lisa was sitting with her in her office, she said, "I need to talk some things through. Maybe you can help me. If we're going to be partners, I don't want to have secrets. I've got some baggage and I'm beginning to see that it's getting in my way."

Lisa nodded. "Well, you know, most of us do."

"Mine is the kind where I toss the man I love, who also happens to be a cop, who also happens to be trying to protect me, out of my apartment. I feel stifled and messed up and…and scared."

She touched Serena on the shoulder. "You're both under a lot of stress. Why don't you tell me what happened?"

It felt so good to unburden herself. To talk to a woman who not only was a colleague but was becoming a friend.

When she'd finished, Lisa said, "Stress makes people do foolish things. Like lash out at the man you love."

"But he was acting so controlling."

"I know. Sounds to me like he's in love with you, too. It was pretty obvious when he came storming in here after they found that woman. He thought at first she was you. I think that's what made him crazy. He's terrified he'll lose you. Afraid he won't be able to protect you."

She hadn't really looked at the situation from Adam's point of view. And it had never occurred to her that he could be in love with her, too.

"It's an impossible situation. If we were a normal couple, we'd date and see each other a couple of times a week. Go to movies and, I don't know, out for dinner. Hang out with each other's friends. Instead we hide out most of the time. Half the time I don't feel like I have his full attention. He's too busy looking over his shoulder, checking doors and windows. Freaking me out."

"I know it's tough. For both of you."

She let out a breath. "I overreacted. And I miss him. What do I do?"

"Take a little time. Calm down. Then I suggest you go and talk to Adam. Let him know some of what you've told me. Why you react so strongly to being controlled. He's a cop. A protector. It's what he does. How he sees himself. He's feeling vulnerable, too. And scared. Maybe you can help each other deal with some stuff from your pasts."

She thought about that. And about the best part of what Lisa had said. "You really think he loves me?"

"Yeah. I do. Hasn't he ever told you?"

She shook her head. "No." She let her breath out in a huff. "Typical male. Won't communicate about his feelings."

"Serena? Have you told Adam how you feel?"

Ouch. Busted. "Not in so many words."

"Maybe it's time."

"Time to tell a man who has control issues that I love him?"

"I don't want to be rude, and remember, I'm speaking here as your pseudopsychologist, not your employee, but you actually have some control issues, too."

It felt good to laugh, even if she was laughing at herself. When was the last time she'd really laughed? "I know."

"Give it a day or two so you can both calm down and get some perspective. Then call Adam. Talk to him."

She narrowed her gaze. "How did you do in psychology, anyway?"

Lisa grinned at her. "I got honors."

IT FELT STRANGE to wake up without Adam beside her the next day. Stranger still to realize she missed him.

She'd barely known him a few weeks and he'd gone

from reluctant client to protector to lover to—she had no idea when it had happened—the man she loved.

Serena knew herself well enough to know she wasn't a woman who fell in love easily. Or, unfortunately, out of it easily.

She also knew Lisa was right. She needed to have a conversation with Adam. Needed to sort through her feelings and explain to him what she couldn't really explain to herself. She was so used to being self-reliant. You didn't need Lisa's degree in psychology to understand that if a child couldn't rely on her mother, she was always going to have a difficult time trusting. And Serena hadn't slowly come to trust Adam by getting to know him and dating and exploring the normal boundaries of a relationship. She'd been thrown into this drama and forced to trust him.

And he was a protector, of course. A man whose natural inclination to boss and control—even in a benign way—he had only strengthened by choosing policing as his career.

Serena struggled to recapture the morning routine that had been so ingrained in her up until a few weeks ago.

Making her formerly daily smoothie in the blender took a little longer since she had to think about the ingredients. She took an extra few seconds to locate her gym socks. How quickly Adam had inserted himself into her life and messed up her careful and extremely efficient routines.

Once she'd pulled herself together, she headed down to her car. She might be stubborn and independent to a fault, but she tried not to be a stupid woman. She chose to believe the young woman's tragic death right in this building had been a coincidence, not a message for her. But Adam could be right.

So she called Mark, let him know she was heading for the gym and that he could expect her in the office at eight-thirty.

"Why don't I come and get you?" he suggested in his nondomineering way, which she appreciated.

"No. I'm fine."

"I'd like to stay on the line with you until you get into your car, if that's all right."

"I was hoping you would."

She lost the signal briefly in the elevator, was able to pick it up again in the lobby and chatted to him as she scanned the garage, checked that there was no one hiding in her car.

She got in, fired up the engine, pulled out of the parking garage.

"Everything's fine, Mark. I'll see you at the office."

"See you then."

She pulled up to the gym and as she emerged from her car, a familiar figure in black pants and a shirt emblazoned with the gym's logo jogged out of the side door. He ran up to her, a gym bag thrown over his shoulder.

"Glad I caught you," Tim said, looking somewhat less like his usual smiling, happy self. "I don't think you should go in there."

An uncomfortable feeling began in the pit of her stomach. Part dread, part irritation. Was there no place she could be free from interfering, overprotective men? "Why not?"

"It's Stan. He's been asking a lot of questions about you. Since he got back from Poland, he's been acting weird."

"Weird? What kind of weird?" Psycho-killer stalker weird?

"I can't really explain it. Just a feeling I get."

Since she'd never confided in her personal trainer about the creepy texts and emails, she had to assume Stanley was, in fact, acting strange and it would be foolish to go into that gym.

"Damn it," she said, half to herself. "I was really looking forward to my workout today. Got some stress I need to relieve."

"I hear you." He paused. Seemed to consider. "Tell you what. I'm not really supposed to do this, but since you're a good client, I'm going to tell you about a private gym I train people in. I'm on my way there now. Why don't you come, check it out. You can do your workout without Stan dribbling in his shorts and, if you like the place, you might want to join."

"Is it far? I need to be back in my office by eight-thirty."

"No. Not far. I can give you a lift. Drop you back here at eight-fifteen."

"Um…" She didn't like driving with other people. She preferred taking her own car. Control issues, Lisa would probably diagnose.

As though reading her mind, he said, "Or we can take your car. You can drop me back here. Parking's a bit dodgy at the other gym. We're working on getting it sorted." He walked around to her passenger side as he talked. Then looked back.

"Better get a move on. Looks like Stanley's on his way out here."

Sure enough, when she glanced back at the gym, a familiar squat figure was watching her out of the window. A wash of horror grabbed at her as she recalled the texts, the emails and those awful faces on her door and in her bed.

The door opened.

"Let's get out of here," she said, popping the locks. She jumped into the driver's seat and Tim settled himself in the passenger side. Stanley emerged from the gym and stared after her as she pulled out into traffic.

She could feel him watching her until she was out of sight.

20

TIM DIRECTED AND she drove, only half paying attention to where they were going. She was thinking she should call Adam and let him know that Stanley was behaving so oddly that other people were starting to notice.

"I'm excited to show you the place," Tim said, intruding on her thoughts.

She decided to put Adam, Stanley and the rest of it out of her mind and enjoy her workout. "I didn't know you had a private gym," she said, moving automatically into business mode. "What's your business model?"

"My training is very private."

"Okay. You mean like elite individuals?"

"Something like that." He sounded as though he was amused. She glanced over at him as the first flutter of unease flickered across her belly. She'd told Mark she was on her way to the gym, but with the rush to get away from Stanley she hadn't updated him on her plans. And here she was alone with a man she didn't know all that well.

Then she scoffed at her own foolishness. That was what happened when you let fear take hold. Tim was her personal trainer. They'd worked together for more than a year.

She followed his directions, turning away toward an

industrial area and in the opposite direction to her office. "I thought you said it was close by?"

"It is. Another couple of minutes. I really value your opinion. I'll give you a quick training session and you can try out the equipment. See what you think."

"All right."

Since they were almost there, she kept going, but she realized that if he hadn't made her so jumpy about Stanley, what she should have done was to go into the gym. There were plenty of people around. She could have made sure someone walked her back to her car.

The gym was more than five extra minutes of driving, by which time she'd already decided it was too far for her to take seriously. And she was going to have to talk to Tim about the ethics of poaching clients from one employer while setting up his own business. Not cool.

As they pulled into a parking lot in front of a squat cement building he said, "Thanks for doing this." He flashed her his big charming smile. "I'm so excited to show you the space. Get your opinion."

And because he'd been a good trainer and given her lots of tips between sessions, she said, "No problem. I need to call the office and tell them where I am and that I'll be back a bit late."

"Sure."

As she picked up the phone, he grabbed her arm. "Quick, get inside." He sounded urgent.

"What?"

"Stanley. He must have followed us here. No, don't look. I don't think he's seen you." And he pulled her urgently toward the door, putting his big body between her and the street.

"But—" She tried to pull away. She was so sick of men telling her what to do. "He'll see my car."

"Come on."

"No." She'd had it. "I'm calling the police."

He still had her cell phone hand clasped tightly in his and the keys to his gym in the other. He had the door opened and shoved them both through the doorway before slamming the door behind them and locking it.

She felt irritable, shaken up and oddly frightened. Adam. She needed to call Adam.

Even as she had the thought, she felt the phone grabbed out of her hand. She gave a hiss of alarm and annoyance. "What are you doing?"

"The way I figure it, we both train people. You train them to conquer fear. I train them to explore every drop of it."

His voice was so odd, his words so bizarre that she turned her head sharply to look at him.

And what she saw made her heart drop to the soles of her feet. In that second he let his mask slip and she saw behind the charming, easygoing Aussie athlete/trainer to the monster within.

"Oh, my God," she said. "It's you."

"Yes, my darling. And it's taken you a bloody long time to work it out. I'm surprised at you. A little disappointed. I thought you were smart." He shook his head sadly. "But you're not smart at all. Never mind. You can still experience fear. And pain. And we're going to have some fun, you and I, forcing you to depths of horror you've never even imagined."

She swallowed. Refused to speak until she was fairly sure there'd be no tremor in her voice. "Why?"

"Why what? Why the personal project? Or why you?"

"Why…both?" If she kept him talking, she'd have a little more time to think.

He chuckled. Chucked her under the chin as though she

were a child. She turned her head away, revolted by his touch. "You think you're going to buy time and keep me talking? Like in the movies, until the cavalry gets here? News flash, girlie. Cavalry isn't coming. Nobody knows where you are."

"Stanley saw us leave together," she reminded him.

"Stanley," he snorted. "You'll be seeing him again. Sooner than you think. Poor old Stan. His horrible infantile crush on you made my work so much easier. A little later you'll call him. Tell him you're stranded. Ask him to meet you here. He'll come because of that horrible crush of his." He shook his head. "Pathetic."

"No," she said. "I won't."

"Yeah," he said. "You will. A couple of hours from now, you'll do anything I ask you to. Anything at all. Pain and fear are remarkable motivators. I've made quite a study." He paused. Glanced around. "When Stanley gets here, I'll let him watch the last bit. He deserves at least that much. And when you're dead—I hope you've understood by now that by nightfall, midnight if you're really strong, you'll be dead—poor old Stan, having murdered you, will naturally kill himself. Nice easy case that even your cop boyfriend could solve."

Her body jerked at that. "I don't have a cop boyfriend."

"Don't play stupid. It doesn't suit you. Did you think I didn't laugh myself silly watching you? You had a cop living in and a rent-a-cop following you at work. I knew the fear was already starting to work. I probably wouldn't have sent you any more messages for a while anyway, simply to watch you all squirm. But Stan went out of the country, so obviously the game had to pause until he returned. Really, his timing couldn't have been better."

"You still haven't answered my question."

"The why?" He shrugged. "It's a hobby, I suppose. A

personal study project. To take someone on this journey is extraordinary. To watch them fight for life and then finally succumb is amazing. Powerful stuff. It's so much better than sex."

"And why me? What have I ever done that you would hate me so much?"

"It's not about hate, darling. You know that. It's about power. You have it. You wield it so effortlessly, telling people how to live without fear. How to build their businesses and fix their sorry inner selves and overcome abuse and blah, blah, blah. When you came to me for training, I knew that on some level you were offering yourself to me. A sacrifice."

"All I wanted was stronger abs and better cardio," she muttered.

ADAM SLEPT LIKE CRAP. He had dreams he didn't want to remember and the rest of the time he brooded. How had he got into this mess? He tried to protect a woman, he fell in love with her and she dumped him.

He was nothing but a cliché.

And he'd stay dumped. No problem there. If she didn't want him, that was fine. But he wouldn't leave Serena in danger. He couldn't.

He made a very large pot of very strong coffee. Gulped down a couple of mugs of the stuff while he showered and shaved. He checked his email. Got one that made him swear viciously and grab his car keys. He got into his car. Called Joey on the way.

"What?" Joey didn't like early calls. He didn't like mornings.

"Stanley Wozniak did not go to Poland."

"What?"

"I did some checking. Found out this morning. He wasn't in Poland for those two weeks."

"Where the hell was he?"

"He was in Mexico. In one of those kinky adult resorts. Holiday camp for perverts."

"Okay, so he lied. Maybe he didn't want people knowing he likes to hang around the pool watching topless girls play water polo or whatever the hell they do at those places. Doesn't mean he sent Serena those messages."

"I'm on my way to Serena's gym. She works out this time of day."

"Adam," the tired voice reminded him, "she dumped your ass. She doesn't want you stalking her."

"Wozniak is the key to this. He has to be," Adam snapped, refusing to get into the stalking issue. He glanced at his watch. "I'll be in the office by eight-thirty."

"Do not harass him. Do you hear me? We do not need a harassment suit."

Adam pulled up to the gym. *Play it cool,* he reminded himself as he got out of the car. She'd be there.

All he was going to do was make his presence obvious. Let Stanley the Stalker know that he was under intense supervision.

He walked into the gym. Flashed his shield at the front desk. Said he'd come to see someone. The young woman at the front waved him through with a nervous smile.

He entered the main gym area. A wall of mirrors on one side multiplied the sweating bodies of indoor cyclists, the odd glide of the elliptical trainer, treadmill runners and walkers. On the other side of the long room a wall of windows reminded the patrons of what they could be doing. Exercising outside. For free.

Serena wasn't in her usual spot. He scanned the full row and didn't spot her.

Stanley. Where was Stanley? He stalked down between the rows of machines and didn't see either of them. Anxiety began to gnaw at his gut but he forced himself to stay calm.

Got to the mat area where she liked to stretch. Beside that was the weight room. Serena was nowhere to be found but he saw Stanley huffing and red-faced as he attempted biceps curls with dumbbells that were clearly too heavy for him.

He appeared miserable and in pain as Adam approached. When he spotted him, Stanley lowered the weights.

"Where's Serena?"

"She went off with that guy." He shook his head. "I don't like it. I went out to try and stop her, but she drove her car like a bat from Hades."

"What guy?"

"The trainer. I see the way he looks at her when she doesn't see. It's not right. I wanted to tell her not to—"

"What trainer?" he yelled.

"The Australian. His name is Tim Patterson."

"You said she went off with him?"

Stanley nodded, looking even more miserable.

"What time was this?"

"Maybe thirty minutes. I do extra workout. I wait for them to come back."

"Did she say where she was going?"

"She never even came inside. He went out to meet her. With a bag. They had some talk and then he got into her car and they drove away."

"It was her car? You're sure?"

"Yes. She was driving."

"Which way did they go when they pulled out of the lot?"

"They turned left."

"Anything else you noticed? Anything at all?"

"Yes. When I wave to her to stop, she pretend not to scc me."

21

He tried her home and her cell. Both went to voice mail. Hearing her calm, beautiful voice on the message hurt him somewhere deep inside. "I'm coming for you, Serena," he said aloud. "Hang on. I'm coming.

"Stan," he said, "I need you to do something for Serena. Find a picture of the trainer. His employee pass, a poster with his picture on it, something. Scan it and send it to these two addresses. Can you do that?"

"Yes, of course."

He gave him a card and scribbled Joey's and Max's email addresses onto it.

Then he ran outside to his car. Adam's next call wasn't to his fellow cops. It was to Max. "Serena's been taken."

"Shit. When?"

"Thirty to forty minutes ago. From her gym."

"Do we know who has her?"

"An Australian. Her personal trainer at the gym. Goes by the name Tim Patterson. Probably fake."

"Right. What do you need from me?"

"Backup. I'm getting a guy to email you a photograph of Patterson. See what you can find out."

"You got it."

Next he called Joey. Kept his voice cool. But every time he said it, the truth was worse. "He's taken her," he said. "Not Stanley Wozniak. Repeat, not Stanley Wozniak. The man we're looking for is an Australian personal trainer going by the name Tim Patterson."

"Are you sure she's been taken?"

"What?" he exploded. "A witness saw her drive away with her trainer."

"Was she under duress? Did the witness see any violence?"

"Virge, a madman's got my girl. I don't have time for this."

"Hey, I'm only suggesting that maybe she went with her trainer for, say, some extra personal training. Maybe they went for a run outside in nature. Who the hell knows? Before you get every police resource out looking for your girlfriend, make sure she's in bona fide trouble. All I'm saying."

"Stanley's sending you a photo. Check him out. Get back to me."

"Stanley? Your witness is Stanley?"

"I gotta go."

"Where are you going?"

"To get my girl."

"You're not the fucking Lone Ranger," Joey said. "You don't even know where she is."

"Yeah. I do." And he clicked off.

And, more thankful than ever before that his old buddy owned a security firm, he fired up the GPS locator. They'd debated telling Serena, but she was so obsessed with her independence that he'd suggested to Max they keep the fact that there were tracking devices in her car and tucked deeply inside her wallet to themselves. He'd figured the chances she'd go somewhere without one or both of those items was slim. They'd figured that if they never needed to track her, then she never had to know.

And if the damn things saved her life, which he prayed mightily they would, then she wouldn't be too pissed. At least, that was the theory.

Right now he'd take her as angry as a swarm of disturbed hornets. He'd take her any way he could get her.

His mind flashed to the pale, lifeless young woman he'd thought for a few bad minutes was Serena. Then he forced the image away. Serena was strong and she was smart. He knew she'd fight with everything she had.

TIM WAS STANDING between her and the door. Which was locked. While he talked, she'd taken stock of her surroundings. Her findings weren't encouraging. The building had most likely been built as a warehouse. The walls were thick cinder block. She'd seen fitness studios converted from warehouses before and the industrial decor was part of the charm. Not only did this warehouse lack charm, it also lacked windows.

There was plenty of fitness equipment scattered around but she had the feeling it had been bought at auction or from a gym that had closed down.

There had to be another entrance. Her gaze darted around, looking. There was a darker area behind some old metal shelving that seemed a likely spot. If she could get there, if she could distract him long enough to make a run for it, she had a chance.

He was fitter than her, of course, stronger and no doubt faster, but she had the whole running-for-her-life thing on her side.

She suspected it evened things out a bit.

"Are you planning to turn this mess into a gym?" she

asked. Keep him talking, she thought, while she searched for a weapon. Or a plan.

"Yes. It's the first of a planned series. I'll have fitness clubs coast to coast."

"That's pretty expensive on a personal trainer's salary."

"I'm more than that, darling. I was in military intelligence."

She blinked. "For the Australian army?"

"Private army. Very private. My expertise is in untraceable communication and moving money around. Also, obviously, without trace. When my employers found out about my, um, hobby, they decided we were no longer a fit. I barely escaped with my life." He shrugged. "Now I've got a new life, a new identity. But I had to leave most of my assets behind."

"So you're broke."

"Let's just say you're going to make a generous business loan." The charming facade was back in place. He shot her his gorgeous grin. "You won't be needing the money. I do love online banking."

Eight-thirty had come and gone, she was certain. Since she hadn't shown up at the office or called, Mark and Lisa would be trying to track her down. On cue, it seemed, her cell phone chimed. Tim glanced at it. "Lisa called." Then he powered off the phone. "Better save the battery. For later. When I want you to make a call."

His tone made her shiver.

At least if she didn't answer her cell, Lisa would know something was wrong. Mark would get hold of Max and Adam.

She couldn't bear to think of Adam. She had to stay strong. No time for wishing she'd done things differently.

"What about that girl? The one who was found dead in the lobby of my building?" Somehow she still hoped that

poor young woman's death had been an unfortunate coincidence. Not in any way connected with her.

Tim looked pained, as though once again she had disappointed him. "You don't really have to ask me that, do
you? I was so careful. I didn't have any fun with her at all,
keeping her all perfect, like, so the stupid cops would think
it was an accident." He chuckled. "I know a dozen ways
to kill someone so it looks like natural causes. Course, in
your case, it will be quite clear that you were murdered."
He stretched out the last word, his twangy accent somehow making it sound even creepier.

He was clearly enjoying himself. Teasing her, letting her
fear build up until he had her so terrified she'd do anything
he asked. But there was something he didn't know about
her. She'd lived in fear as a child, and she'd become pretty
damned good at triumphing over that emotion.

She might not be physically stronger, but she was both
emotionally stronger and, clearly, more sane.

It wasn't much, but she took what comfort she could
from that. If she could make people more powerful as a
performance coach, maybe she could also work the opposite way. Push him so far into his weakness and psy-
chosis that he snapped.

Tormenting a madman was probably a terrible plan,
but at the moment it was all she had.

Unless she could escape.

She still had her purse hanging over her arm.

As weapons went it wasn't much. But it was something.

Now all she needed was a distraction. A moment of
inattention.

Maybe she could make him mad, get him off balance
that way. "Did your mother hate you?" she asked in a con-
descending tone. "Did your father beat you?" His nostrils

flared but that was all the reaction he showed. "Or were you born evil?"

He took a step forward. Oh, yeah, she'd riled him, all right. His eyes were wild; he was letting his crazy out. She tensed herself, and, like a gift, another cell phone chirped. His, presumably. It was the moment she needed. He turned for his bag and she swung her purse with every bit of strength she possessed.

It hit him in the face and with a huff he fell back.

She was already running away from the main door, hoping against hope that the dim section on the other side of the warehouse hid a second exit.

It did. As she drew closer, she could see it, metal, door shaped. Yes!

And locked from the inside with huge rusty bolts.

"Really, Serena, must you be so tedious?"

He didn't bother running. He strolled toward her. He'd even taken the time to take a gun out from wherever he'd had it hidden.

Her heart sank. The gun gave him an edge she really wished he didn't have. She didn't waste time with the big old bolts. There had to be something. A weapon of some kind.

Amazingly, in the corner, a few pieces of junk metal. And a mousetrap. She ducked, grabbed a sharp-looking twist of metal. And the trap.

He stopped about six feet away. She was breathing heavily from her short sprint. The sound was loud in the empty building. "Come on out, now, or I'll shoot you."

"No, you won't." If she'd learned anything about him from his sick game, it was that he liked cat and mouse. "That would end the game too soon."

She caught the smile that crossed his mouth. "True." He paused. They stared at each other. She could smell the dust she'd kicked up and the musty smell of the old equipment. "I tell you what, I'll shoot that mousetrap out of your hand."

As he said the words, she dropped the thing out of her right hand and leaped to the left. The gunshot blasted by her, thudding into the cinderblock.

"Much better." He closed in. Grabbed her right arm. She let him see fear, let him think he had her. She even managed to whimper.

"Don't hurt me, please," she whispered, her gaze on his. When she saw the satisfaction in his eyes and felt him relax, she frantically tried to think of a way to use the sharp metal and escape without giving him time to shoot her.

ADAM RECOGNIZED HER car in the lot of an old warehouse. The second GPS told him she was inside. He was the first man there. He knew Max would have a team on their way. He paused, knowing he'd be only a danger to Serena if he blasted in alone, as Joey had warned.

He called his partner. Gave him the location and that Serena was inside with Patterson. "You got anything on him yet?"

"Adam, this is a seriously bad dude. Do not approach him, do you understand? He's wanted for crimes that would make you sick."

The knowledge didn't surprise him, only strengthened his resolve.

"He's got Serena."

"Hang on. We're on our way. Five minutes, tops."

He didn't want to imagine the things a sadistic killer could do to a woman in five minutes.

He pulled out his piece, ran the circumference of the place. Two doors. No windows.

He tried easing open the main door, but it was locked. Thought about trying the other door. Because it was stupid not to try the obvious way in first.

Heard a shot from inside.

He stood back. Shielded his face with his arm and fired at the front door lock. Behind him he heard vehicles arriving. Turned to find Max emerging from a paramilitary vehicle with four guys in black wearing helmets and carrying some serious firepower. Max had clearly uncovered the same information that Joey had.

"Shots fired inside," he snapped.

Max gave his firearm a look that clearly said, "Seriously?"

Motioned to his team. A couple of shots from a high-powered rifle and the door lock was history. He figured they would have blasted right through the walls except that with Serena inside they were being careful.

He didn't wait for the smoke to clear. He kicked open what was left of the door and ran inside.

AND SAW HER, in the clutches of a madman with a gun but clearly unharmed.

She was alive. It was all he cared about. She was alive.

Their eyes met across the warehouse and he felt the love burn in his throat. "Hang on," he said with his eyes. "Just hang on."

The guy had a gun and the moment he saw Max's team come crashing through the door behind Adam, he made a move, tried to pull Serena in front of him. It was as though she'd been waiting for that moment. She made a move of her own, jabbing something into the guy's side.

He howled with pain and jumped instinctively away. Serena leaped in the other direction. Good for her.

It was all Adam needed. "Drop the weapon. Now!"

Behind him were four guys in black with enough fire-power to take over a small country.

The bloodlust was so strong he wished Patterson would make a move so he could blow his head off.

Instead, like the coward he was, he dropped the weapon.

"Put your hands on your head," ordered the leader of Max's private troop.

Adam ran for Serena. She ran for him.

As he wrapped his arms around her he knew he'd never let her go again.

"Are you all right?" Stupid thing to say but it was all that came out.

"Yes."

"I love you so much," he said, holding her so tight he could feel her trembling. Or maybe that was his own trembling.

"I love you, too."

He kissed her because he had to. A deep, life-affirming "everything's okay now" kiss that was all the sweeter because he knew how close he'd come to losing her.

When he turned around, Joey was there with half a dozen uniforms in riot gear. "You okay?" his partner asked.

"Yeah. Take over here."

Joey sent a glance at Max's team. "Friends of yours?"

"Yeah. I don't think their involvement needs to be official."

"Right."

When the cops took over the scene, Max and his team disappeared like mist on a hot day.

He put Serena in his car and they headed away. She rubbed her arms. "Do I need to make a statement or fill out a report or something?"

"Later. We'll get to it later."

"Cutting through red tape is just one reason I'm glad I'm in love with a cop," she said, giving him a smile that made his heart melt.

22

ADAM GRABBED HIS gear for the last regular game of the season before play-offs started. "Look, you don't have to come. Why don't you stay in bed?"

Serena stretched her spectacular body and said, "Because I've barely been out of this bed in days."

"You complaining?"

Her chuckle was low and deliciously dirty. "Not hardly."

Amazingly, he could feel himself stirring with desire. He'd have thought he'd be all used up, but she only had to stretch her naked body and he was ready to go again. He moved to the side of the bed. "Maybe we've got time for one more." Then her hand wrapped around him and he couldn't think anymore.

THERE WAS GREAT energy among the Hurricanes. Apart from Dylan being pissed that Adam and Max had brought down an international criminal without him, the team was pretty pumped.

Adam glanced over during warm-up and saw his parents sitting with Serena. He felt as though everything in his world had clicked into place. If his mom were to ask him right now on camera who he was going to marry, he'd have an answer ready.

That strange guilty feeling was nowhere in sight. Serena had helped him see that he wasn't trying to be better than his dad by winning hockey games. He was simply playing his best as part of a team. As his father always had as a cop.

When he recalled how he'd struggled against having a performance coach, he shook his head at his own stubbornness and stupidity. She'd changed every aspect of his life for the better. Damn, she was good.

The win was really pretty unexciting. The Hurricanes were so pumped it would have taken a better team than the Portland Paters to beat them tonight. When they came off the ice, Adam, Dylan and Max made their way to where their scatter of friends and families sat.

Serena and his folks already had a good relationship, and he could see they'd been chatting through the game like old friends.

"I still can't believe what you kids pulled off," his dad said, sounding as proud as could be.

"You mean the win tonight? That was nothing."

The old man shook his head. "I mean arresting one of the most wanted men in the world." He shook his head. "You do the department proud, son. You too, Max."

"One thing I don't understand," Serena said suddenly, "is how you found me so fast." He realized that he'd kept her so busy naked in his bed that they'd barely talked about what had happened. He suspected both of them needed to dwell on more positive things. And sex with Serena was about the most positive thing he'd ever experienced in his life.

He and Max exchanged glances, and Max clearly let him know that since she was his girlfriend, he could tell her.

"Actually, we put a tracking device on your car. Just in case."

"You put a GPS on my car and didn't tell me?"

"In the mood you were in you'd have pried it off and driven over it to piss me off."

"I installed it myself when I first got involved," Max said, taking part of the heat after all. "Adam and I thought it would be a good idea." Neither of them mentioned the one in her wallet, which he'd already removed.

"It would have been nice to know, when I was in the clutches of a deranged psychotic sadist, that my good friends had a way to find me," Serena said. But there wasn't much heat behind her complaint. He guessed that rescuing her from the clutches of said deranged psychotic sadist was probably reasonable payback.

"Next time I'm sure the boys will tell you, dear," his mother said matter-of-factly. And they all laughed.

"It was a terrific game, boys," she said. "I took lots of footage. You know, I can take movies with my new phone. It's amazing."

"Hey," Dylan said, "get out your phone again, June, and ask Adam on film who he's going to marry."

"Dylan," Max said in a warning tone.

"What? It'll be great footage for your sixtieth birthday party. Just sayin'."

"Go ahead, Mom. Do it," he said.

"Oh, honey," she said, getting a little damp around the eyes. "I couldn't be happier."

"Wait," Dylan interrupted. "On camera. I want evidence."

"You suck," Max said.

June got out her smartphone, pushed a few buttons and then said, "Adam, who are you going to marry when you grow up?"

"I, Adam Shawnigan, am going to marry Serena Long, the greatest woman, and the finest performance coach, I've ever met. If she'll have me."

Serena, who'd been watching and listening without saying a word, now said, "Oh, Adam."

He continued, because it felt right that all the people he cared about should know what was in his heart. "You fixed things in me I didn't know were broken, and you taught me what real forever love is." He got down on one knee and damn near fell on his face because of the skates and all the padding, but he recovered. "Serena Long, will you marry me?"

"Oh, Adam, yes, I will marry you. I love you so much. I may have fixed your life, but you saved mine. I'm happy to give you all of it that's left."

"Where's the ring, stupid?" Dylan demanded, sounding way too much like the brat he'd been at five years old.

"This was unplanned," he said.

"You can't get engaged without a ring," Dylan insisted.

"Who made you editor in chief of *Modern Bride?*" Max demanded.

"Wait, I've got an idea. Hold on." Dylan ran up the bleachers in his socks. He emerged in less than two minutes with a plastic ring from the charity vending machine in the rink lobby. "I had to put in three dollars before I got a ring," he complained. "But it's a beaut."

It was, too. Bright purple plastic with a big shiny chunk of glitter on the top.

Serena put out her left hand. June got the phone filming again.

Adam slipped the gaudy plastic ring on her finger. "I'll get you a better one." Then he thought about her control issues. "In fact, we'll pick it out together."

"I'll always treasure this one. But thanks."

"I also have a black plastic tarantula," Dylan said, waving the thing around. "And a whistle."

"I couldn't be happier," June said, hugging Serena.

Adam and his father shook hands, then went in for a man hug.

Max took his turn hugging Serena.

Dylan said, "I couldn't be happier, either. You totally lost the bet!" And he bumped fists with Max. "To the last man standing." And he blew the red plastic whistle.

"You know what, guys?" Adam said, looking at the woman he was going to marry and seeing his future shine back at him from her bright eyes. "I totally won."

* * * * *

COMING NEXT MONTH FROM

HARLEQUIN Blaze

Available February 18, 2014

#787 CAPTIVATE ME
Unrated!
by Kira Sinclair

What is it about Mardi Gras that makes everyone lose their mind? When Alyssa Vaughn notices a masked stranger watching her undress through her bedroom window, the Bacchus attitude takes over. But wait until she finds out who he is!

#788 TEXAS OUTLAWS: COLE
The Texas Outlaws
by Kimberly Raye

Cole Chisholm's love life is even wilder than the horses he rides. When Nikki Barbie asks him to pretend to be her boyfriend, he agrees...but only if some wild, wicked nights are included!

#789 ALONE WITH YOU
Made in Montana
by Debbi Rawlins

Alexis Worthington is smart, ambitious and has a wild streak that alienated her from her family. Now's her chance to prove herself to them. But working with rodeo rider Will Tanner—she's finding it difficult to behave!

#790 UNEXPECTED TEMPTATION
The Berringers
by Samantha Hunter

Luke Berringer thinks he's finally put his past to rest when he catches the woman who ruined his life—but in Vanessa Grant has he actually found the woman who will heal his heart?

HBCNM0214

REQUEST YOUR FREE BOOKS!
2 FREE NOVELS PLUS 2 FREE GIFTS!

HARLEQUIN

Blaze®

red-hot reads!

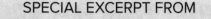
Captivate Me

Amid the revelry of Mardi Gras, Beckett Kayne just wanted a moment of peace. He was enjoying the solitude when a light snapped on in the apartment across the alley.

She stood, framed by the window. A soft radiance lit her from behind, painting her in an ethereal splash of color that made her seem dreamy and tragic and somehow unreal.

Maybe that was why he kept watching. Logically, he realized he was intruding, but there was something about her....

Her eyelids slid closed and her head tipped back. Exhaustion was stamped into every line of her body, but that didn't detract from her allure. In fact, it made Beckett want to reach out and hold her. To take her weight and the exhaustion on himself.

Her hands drifted slowly up her body, settling at the top button of her blouse. With sure fingers, she popped it open. And another. And another. The edge of her red-hot bra came into view revealing an enticing swell of skin.

Tension snapped through Beckett's body. The hedonistic pressure of the night must have gotten to him, after all. Because, even as his brain was screaming at him to give her privacy, he couldn't do it.

It had been a very long time since any woman had pulled this kind of immediate physical reaction from him.

Perhaps it was the air of innocence not even the windowpane and ten feet of alley could camouflage. She was simply herself—unconsciously sensual.

Shifting, Beckett dropped his foot and settled his waist against the edge of the balcony railing. He wanted to be the one uncovering her soft skin. Running his fingers over her body. Hearing the hitch of her breath when he discovered a sensitive spot.

Maybe it was his movement that caught her attention. Suddenly her head snapped sideways and she looked straight into his eyes.

Her fingers stilled. Surprise, embarrassment and anger flitted across her face before finally settling into something darker and a hell of a lot more sinful.

Her arms stretched wide. She undulated, rolling her hips and ribs and spine in a way that begged him to touch.

And then the blinds snapped down between them.

Pick up CAPTIVATE ME by Kira Sinclair, available in March 2014 wherever you buy Harlequin® Blaze® books.

Get ready for a wild ride!

Cole Chisholm's love life is even wilder than the horses he rides. When Nikki Barbie asks him to pretend to be her boyfriend, he agrees...but only if some wild, wicked nights are included.

Pick up the final chapter of
The Texas Outlaws miniseries

Texas Outlaws: Cole
by *USA TODAY* bestselling author
Kimberly Raye

AVAILABLE FEBRUARY 18, 2014,
wherever you buy Harlequin Blaze books.

HARLEQUIN®

Blaze®

Red-Hot Reads
www.Harlequin.com

HB79792

Welcome to Last Bachelor Standing!

How long can three sexy single men hold out?

First up? Mr. No Commitment...Detective Adam Shawnigan.
As you can see, ladies, he has the protective cop hero thing
happening—plus he's all gorgeous height, piercing dark
eyes, sensuous mouth and lean hot body. But here comes
sweet temptation....

 Long is helping Adam prepare for
urns out, he's also in a position
roblem. It's quid pro quo, both
in the bedroom and the bets—and the bedroom
games—are on!

$5.50 U.S./$6.25 CAN.

ISBN-13: 978-0-373-79789-9

50550

9 780373 797899

EAN

S